CLICK

By Briana Michaels

Copyright

Dedication

For those who like them big and growly —
may the chase be wild, the capture be thrilling,
and the orgasms make you scream
until your throat is raw.

Author's Note

Please don't use this, or any other book of mine, as an educational tool. It might be inspiring, but always play responsibly and do your research. I take creative liberties because this is a work of fiction and I'm a chaotic creature in all aspects of my life.

Thank you for reading!

Chapter 1

Carson

"Arch your back a little more. That's it, now stay just like that for me. Fucking perfect." I snap several pics and work my way around the bed. "Don't move."

"But I can't hold it much longer."

"Yes, you can." I kneel at the foot of the bed. "Bring your right knee up a little closer to your core. That's it. Perrrrfect." I snap another series of shots and back away with a smile on my face. "Okay, we're done."

My client sighs with relief as her arms and legs flop down when she relaxes on the bed. "You weren't kidding about needing to stretch first." She flexes her arms and rolls over onto her belly. "I'm gonna be sore all day from this."

"I did warn you." Not all poses are simple—especially the ones that make the best pics later.

"So..." Her brow knits together with insecurity and curiosity. "How do they look?"

"Incredible." I don't need to check my

camera to know these pics are fire. I'm damn good at my job and have an eye for the best possible turnout. While my client gets herself untangled from the bedsheets, I tuck my lenses away, and am already mentally preparing for my next client. "You did fantastic, Aubrey. Your wife is going to love these."

"Can I take a peek?"

"Absolutely." It's no sweat off my balls if someone wants to see a couple of their photos prematurely. In fact, I encourage them because it'll only solidify the fact that they didn't waste their money on me. "Later this weekend I'll run them through edits and should have the proofs to you by the end of the month."

"That's super fast."

Overworked and underfucked has become my new lifestyle, but if I don't stay busy, I'll go insane. "Unless something major goes wrong, like a zombie apocalypse, I always try to have a quick turnaround." Sleep is for the weak.

Tipping my camera screen, I let her look at a few shots and stare at her face, loving her expression. Most clients' reactions are the same when they see what they look like through a camera lens—surprise usually hits first, then a little embarrassment, and last, but not least, is confidence.

I live for those looks.

"Wow, Carson. You're seriously talented." Aubrey pulls her flaming red hair into a low ponytail.

"All I did was point and click. You did all the work." I turn the camera off and place it on the table. "Your hair caught the light just right in that last set, it looked like fire."

"You said it would." Slapping my shoulder, she gives it a squeeze and adds, "You're worth every penny, man. This is going to make a great anniversary gift."

I smile and try to relax. I'm not a fan of being touched. It's something I'm always working on. At least it's my shoulder she's gripping and not something worse.

Once she leaves to get changed, I remake the bed and start setting up for the next photoshoot.

"Hey!" My assistant, Chloe, calls out from the doorway. "You want anything delivered for lunch?"

"Nah." I brought mine. "You get yourself something and put it on my card. And uhhh..." I look at the clock and realize my next client will be here in about twenty minutes. "Can you bring in some more waters for me, please?"

"No prob, boss."

Once Chloe leaves, I move my lights and filters and all the other shit that comes with being a boudoir photographer around the huge studio. Thank fuck this next session will be shorter, and easier, than this current one.

"Thanks again, Carson!" Aubrey comes out

of the dressing room and hoists her duffel bag filled with outfits higher onto her shoulder. "It was a real pleasure to meet you."

"It was great meeting you too, Aubrey." I walk over to shake her hand. Handshakes I can do, especially when I'm the one initiating them. I'm all about control. "And congrats on your ten-year anniversary."

My cell goes off in my back pocket. Aubrey waves goodbye and I do the same as I pull my phone out and answer it. "Cruz Photography."

"Hi, yes. This is Mak. Uhh… Makayla. Makayla Johnson."

"Hi Makayla."

"Yeah, Hi. Umm." There's a lot of shuffling in the background and the sound of something breaking. "I have to cancel tomorrow. My appointment's at eleven."

"I'm sorry you have to cancel, but if you want to reschedule, I gotta warn you, I'm booked out for the next eighteen months." I probably sound like a pompous dick saying that, but a lot of times people change their mind, or life happens, and they think they can just come back in a week or two and get annoyed when that's not possible.

"Oh no. I won't be rescheduling."

For some reason, that bugs the shit out of me. "Can I ask why?" I know it's none of my business, but sometimes my mouth runs faster than my professionalism.

"This was supposed to be a gift to my ex, and we broke up a while ago. No sense in coming now, you know? God, he's such a dick." More crashing noises echo in the background. "A selfish, egotistical, narcissistic piece of shit." More crashing. "Judgy twatful." *Crash!* "No good twatermelon." *Bang! Smash!*

"Sounds like a real twatopotamus."

"Oh, he is. Was." *Smash!* "A super big cuntaloupe."

I can't stop myself from laughing.

"Glad you're amused," she says, and giggles a little too.

Smash!

"What is all that noise?"

"Therapy," she huffs. "Anyway, sorry for taking up your time, but yeah, I'm still cancelling."

My gut clenches with guilt. I have a no refund policy on the down payment my clients make when they book an appointment with me, but I feel a little bad for sticking to that rule sometimes. Like now. "I'm sorry, but I don't do refunds."

And a quick glance at my laptop shows me she's prepaid for the session already. In. Full.

"That's okay. It was clear on the form the sessions were non-refundable. Maybe put it towards someone else's if that's a thing. Like a pay it forward but with bomb-ass pics or whatever. Upgrade their package or something with it. Or keep it for yourself and pay bills, get a tattoo. Not that you have tattoos. I mean, you might, it's not like I would know, but I'm just saying, you could go out to a steak dinner or something with it."

This woman is, by far, one of the chattiest people I've ever had the pleasure of talking to. She sounds adorable.

"Come in anyway." I know I should break my business code, give her the money back, and cut my losses, but something about this woman is starting to fascinate me. "You might as well take revenge pics. You've already paid for the session anyway, right?"

Her laugh makes my dick hard. "Yeah, like he'd ever be lucky enough to see photos of me in these outfits."

"All the more reason to keep your appointment with me. Do it for yourself, not him. The best part of revenge is when you get it without blatantly shoving their nose in it. Moving on like he means nothing to you is goddess-level vengeance in my opinion."

She's suddenly quiet on the other line. Shit, did we get disconnected?

"Mak?"

"Um… Yeah?" Her voice sounds sweet like honey.

"See you at eleven tomorrow."

Chapter 2

I have no idea what I'm doing.

After hanging up with the photographer, I stare at the shattered glass filling the recycling bin and the amount of satisfaction I feel about it should come with a warning: Watch out, may make you wet.

Actually, breaking my ex's beer and shot glass collection has nothing to do with why I'm so worked up right now. That photographer got me this way, and he didn't even do anything but tell me to show up tomorrow for my appointment.

That's it.

He didn't even call me a good girl, or say anything really hot at all. He just told me to show up for my prepaid session and I'm soaked.

Wow, Mak, you really need to get laid.

Easier said than done. After breaking up with my boyfriend eight months ago, I've had an itch that I just can't seem to scratch. To make things more miserable, I still can't get him out of my life. He's like mold. Right when I think I've cleared his existence out of my world, I look again and find a spot I missed—like when I just stubbed my toe on a box filled with brewery glasses in my spare bedroom.

He-who-shall-not-be-named-because-he's-a-total-cuntcake keeps saying he'll pick up the rest of his shit and still hasn't. I'm not a damn storage unit and I've reached the end of my rope. We may be over, but I'm still paying for the mistake of agreeing to move in with him. I can't get out of this apartment lease—the one he insisted we co-sign even after I said I hated it here—for another two months.

After accidentally kicking and nearly tripping over this box of useless glassware, I'd sat on the edge of the bed and pulled my phone out to call my bestie. Instead, I got sidetracked with my email and saw the reminder from Cruz Photography saying they couldn't wait to see me tomorrow and even sent a list of what to expect and things to bring for my eleven o'clock shoot.

I'd completely forgotten about it, honestly.

Goddamnit, I want nothing more than to put the past behind me, but it keeps sneaking back up in stupid ways that makes me rage. So much money wasted on that asshole. So much time and energy.

So, like any spiteful, efficient woman, I'd decided to kill two birds with one move—I called the photographer as I grabbed the box of glassware so I could take care of both at the same time. Then I dropped the stupid box just before my call was answered and the sound of glass breaking gave me a great, wonderful, awful idea.

That's when I broke every single one of these stupid souvenirs from the brewery tours He-who-is-a-jerk-face dragged me to. I wasn't lying when I told the photographer it was therapy. It felt amazing to break all this shit. Freeing, really, because now my ex has no reason to come back to my place and grab it.

Not that he was going to anyway.

Now here I am, one box lighter, one possibly broken toe later, and a boudoir session planned for tomorrow with a man who legit made my pussy clench when he said my name.

Holy moly, how's that even possible? I really need to get laid if I'm so bad off that one little order from a stranger has me this horny right now. It's positively shameful.

Trudging back up the steps to my apartment, I do a little self-reflection. All that guy did was take control. Tell me what to do. I'm not sure why I even liked it.

Okay, maybe it was his talk of low-key revenge and having goddess-level vengeance. Or was it his tone?

Actually, now that I'm overthinking it, I'd say it was the entire conversation—from the *cuntaloupe* to the *see you at eleven tomorrow*. As if I have no other place to be except in his studio, on the business end of his camera… in my panties.

And I couldn't say no.

I didn't want to.

A self-love boudoir session might be just the thing for me. Why stop at the photoshoot, right? There are plenty of things I've been wanting to do for myself and haven't yet. Today is a new me. Might as well go all in and grab my fantasies by the balls and give it a good tug.

Or is it grab life by the hair and give it a good tug?

Whatever. I'll do both.

I'm about to carpe this motherfucking diem.

Today is the day. This is it. I'm officially going to take the next step in my self-discovery journey. Tomorrow is boudoir, but today? Today is all about finding a Dom to play with.

I said what I said.

Chewing on my bottom lip, I whip out my cell and open the app, K!nkLink.

Leaning against my kitchen counter for support, my fingers shake as I finally fill out the rest of the registration process that's been sitting as *incomplete* for months. I've agonized over this fetish site for months, and now I'm doing it.

Goddess-level status, here I come.

There's so much to fill out, from gender to honorifics to hard limits, soft limits, curiosities, and all the other things that make me squirm when I think about them. I'm not sure what to put for some of the boxes, so I say *No Preference,* and move on.

Jeez, there're a lot of questions on here. It's overwhelming. Fifteen minutes later, I'm finally almost to the finish line.

Final step: *Please upload a profile pic.*

Snapping a quick selfie, I upload the damn thing without giving myself time to overthink it and my belly somersaults when I click on the confirmation and put in my verification code.

The screen changes and I swear I feel like Alice falling down a rabbit hole filled with whips, chains, and paddles while I wait for it to give me the green light.

Welcome to K!nkLink!

Holy shit, I'm in.

I have no clue how this is going to go, but from what I've read, this is the best and safest site to use. Excitement races through me as I scroll through different profiles, kink lists, chats, and educational tabs. There's a lot to read about and explore, but the knot in my stomach eases because I feel more confident about my decision to take this leap when I see how thorough this app is.

I've spent the better part of six months teetering on whether to join something like this or continue down the road of videos and spicy books to figure out what I like and don't like.

Being inspired by what I read in my beloved smut books has been great—authors have a lot of imagination—but reading about it and getting turned on, and experiencing it firsthand, are *not* the same sometimes. I've been scared to dive into what I find most alluring, and I want a partner who knows what they're doing because I'm not experienced enough.

One of the billion reasons He-who-is-a-dipshit and I didn't work out was because he never listened to what I wanted and the few times he tried to "entertain" my fantasies, he nearly turned them into nightmares.

But on this site, seeing I'm not alone with what turns me on, I feel seen and understood.

Primal is the one thing that really revs me up. I like rough sex. I love the idea of being chased. I want to be forced to the ground and ravished. I want a man growling in my ear, dominating me and fucking me so good I can't walk the next day.

Damn, I'm wet just thinking about it.

My heart races as I scroll through different profiles, comparing my tastes with theirs. Everyone is different, and even though I'm not much for some of these kinks, I'd be willing to try most of them at least once.

I think.

Probably.

One profile in particular catches my interest immediately: **WolfByte.**

Okay, that name is cheesy as fuck. I love it.

Clicking on their profile, a gorgeous man

with black hair and brown eyes stares back at me. He has snakebite piercings on his bottom lip. *Yes. Please.* I smash his *Kinklist* button so fast, it's a miracle I don't crack my phone screen. The first word on their very long list is PRIMAL.

My mouth waters.

Checking out the rest of his profile, I don't really know what some of it means, but I'll google all the kink terms later. I tap on his picture again. Too bad I can't see the rest of his body, but if it's half as hot as his face, then I'm a goner. Before chickening out, I send him a wink.

OMG, I just did it. I initiated the first move. *Go me!*

This small act feels really empowering. I'm taking charge of what I want in a lover and I'm so proud of myself for taking this leap. Doing something like this is scary and, honestly, probably a little dangerous too. Jumping onto a fetish site requires caution, but tonight, I'm sick of being careful, I want to be wild.

K!nkLink Bot: WolfByte would like to chat. Do you consent?

I stare at the two bubbles that pop up—green for yes, red for no.

Holy shit. *Okay, play it cool, Mak. You got this.*

I hit the green bubble and a chat screen opens.

WolfByte: ...

I wait impatiently for the little dots to stop

moving, then I realize the three little dots are all he's sent me. What the hell?

Pricurious: Hi.

WolfByte: You're new.

Pricurious: Is it that obvious?

I mean, damn, I just logged in. What is this guy, a gatekeeper or stalker or something?

WolfByte: The little pink dot on your profile marks you as new.

Oh. Well, never mind then.

Pricurious: Oh. Right. And here I thought my stalker fantasies were about to come to life with the first dude I meet online.

WolfByte: You like being stalked?

Pricurious: Don't know. Hasn't happened yet.

My hands are already clammy and my heart's kicking against my chest.

Pricurious: What does the purple dot on your profile mean?

WolfByte: I'm vetted.

That's interesting. I wonder if this app will only let me see vetted members, and that's why he was one of the first to catch my eye? WolfByte then sends me a link to the color-coded system K!nkLink uses.

Ohhhh, this is good. I'm feeling a little less confused now.

Pricurious: Thanks. I had no idea there were so many color dots and meanings.

I chew on my bottom lip, waiting for him

to say something more. When he doesn't, I start feeling awkward. Crap, did he leave the chat already?

Pricurious: You still there?

WolfByte: Pri… curious. What does that mean to you?

So much for thinking my handle was clever.

Pricurious: I'm into Primal. And I'm curious.

It's pretty much the truth. I love the idea of primal play. I just haven't had a chance to fulfill that fantasy yet, hence the *curious* part of my handle. But the thought of being chased through the woods and fucked within an inch of my life is a wet dream I want to come true.

WolfByte: You like breath play?

I smile.

Pricurious: Yes.

WolfByte: Cum play?

Pricurious: Yes.

WolfByte: Biting and scratching?

Pricurious: Yes and yes.

I can't tell if he's looking up my favorite things on my kink list or just guessing as he goes. It almost feels like he's verifying what I have listed instead of taking my profile at my word. I don't mind. I should probably do the same with him, considering his list is way longer than mine. It makes me even more curious and eager to play with this guy.

WolfByte: Are you taken?

I frown.

Pricurious: ???

WolfByte: I don't share my meals. Do you have a partner?

Holy crap. Am *I* the meal? My cheeks heat at the idea of being eaten… *by a wolf.*

Cue the over-the-top Little Red Riding Hood fantasies.

Pricurious: No.

Waiting with bated breath for him to say something else, another notification pops up. Clicking on it, my heart stops as I read:

K!nkLink: WolfByte *has sent you a contract to play! A copy has been sent to the email linked to this account. Please play responsibly and remember, consent and safety are key to having fun.*

O. M. G.

My hands shake as I send him a response.

Pricurious: That was fast.

I'm too nervous to say more. I'm already making a list of a million scenarios and honestly, I almost want to close my account. I dove into this thinking I could go slow and wade through the waters of this lifestyle, but getting sent a contract within minutes already makes me feel pressured and in over my head.

But I wanted this, right? And I'm a woman who will easily talk herself out of anything that's even remotely scary, even if the chances are good that I'll love it.

WolfByte: Look it over. Take your time deciding. We can adjust as needed for both of us. Everything is negotiable, Pricurious.

I don't even have enough sense to respond at this point. Panicking, I close out of the app and toss my phone on the bed like it's going to bite me.

Holy shit. What am I about to get myself into?

Chapter 3

Carson

Patience is something I have in spades. I love the chase, the hunt, the anticipation that comes beforehand and the satisfaction that thrums in my system after it's all over. But I have to admit, I'm anxious to hear back from Pricurious. Her kink list matched mine in a lot of ways and I'm dying for a taste of her. If we're half as compatible in person as we are on that app, then this is going to be a fuck ton of fun for us both.

Still, I refuse to get my hopes too high. She seems too good to be true, and in my experience, there's always a catch.

After a brisk walk in the woods behind my house, where I imagine what it would be like to hunt, chase, and catch a pretty little bunny girl with dark hair and gorgeous body and fuck her until she screams, I head back inside my house for a cold shower but not before grabbing my cell from the kitchen table and checking to see if she's replied yet.

If Pricurious has any sense, she better take

her time going over my contract. And if she's already signed it, I'll have a lot of work to do because she's made her decision too fast, which may create problems for us later. Then again, one might call me a hypocrite for being hasty with my offer.

Whatever. I know exactly what I'm doing. My carefully constructed rules have been fine-tuned over the years, and I know exactly what it takes to make a dynamic like this function best. I'm not as expert level as some of my friends, but after being a part of the kink community for a few years now, I'm definitely a pro.

This lifestyle takes research, experience, and acute awareness. While in college, I finally embraced the things that made my blood rush and dick hard, then learned all I could to make what I like enjoyable for others too. I've been in a lot of circles, worked with a lot of people, and this app is definitely one of the best ones out there. That doesn't mean you still don't get shitheads now and then who try to register just to get their rocks off on being abusive, untethered alphaholes. Or the newbies who get in over their head and have a really bad experience because they signed up for something they just weren't prepared for yet. Caution trumps confidence in my world.

Being vetted was a long, thorough process, and the fact that the developer of this app took the time to be so meticulous about how they selected the few Doms who have a purple dot on their profile is the only reason I'm still a member.

That, and I'm friends with the guy who developed it.

Look, there's a lot that goes into this type of lifestyle. Games and scenes played out between consenting adults can become really fucking intense. It's important to have trust and good communication. It's also imperative that a newbie is paired with a vetted member until they're ready to go to the next level in their sexual journey.

I usually partner with someone and stay with them for anywhere between three months to a year. My tastes need to match theirs, and any adjustments we make for each other are hashed out ahead of time, and in great detail.

Safe words, soft limits, hard limits — those are generally easy to come up with. But if you're new, like Pricurious, well, I don't always trust what they have listed on their profile. Sometimes they put kinks down that they *think* they like but mark them as absolute favorites. It might be true, but sometimes it isn't. Regardless of the warnings and clear notifications during the registration process, some people still put kinks down on their list as if they're experts in that field when they've never tried them at all. It's a dangerous move for all involved.

And even if they do like a certain kink,

they might have different feelings when they're in the moment. That's okay, too. It happens all the time. Just one more reason why it's important to have a trusted expert to play with.

My contract is basic enough to lay some ground rules, but has plenty of room for negotiation and discussion. I tailor it to suit my sub's needs and desires, while still fulfilling a few of my own.

Like with many relationships, even this kind of situationship can evolve.

It can also die out.

No matter where this leads, I'm going to have a talk with Pricurious about precautions and strict rules, so that even when she's out of my hands, and onto another Dom, she won't be fresh meat on the kink market for a true predator to pounce on.

That contract I sent her states that we will be honest with each other and open about our desires. It also says that neither of us can have another partner, so long as our relationship is intact, and the length of time will be discussed and agreed upon once the initial basics are hashed out.

Once she signs it, she'll be my new partner.

It also makes her my prey.

Primal is my number one kink, and it's the only thing that really gets me off. If she agrees to it, she'll be in for a treat, and I'll finally be able to work off some of the stress that's built up inside me for the past few months.

My body needs a release. I usually keep myself busy, up to my eyeballs with photoshoots, art shows, networking, and hanging with friends, but I'm also drained, too tense, and fucked in the head to concentrate lately.

A nice prowl in the woods, a chase, and hard fuck will set me straight.

Funny, I haven't been on *K!nkLink* for months. Not since my last contract ended this past summer. It was a fun run, but she and I didn't mesh like I'd hoped and, honestly, I got bored fast. I think she did too. There was no fight. No spark. Nothing.

Then again, I haven't felt a spark since…

Don't go there. It'll just drag you back down, and you don't need that right now.

The idea of making Pricurious my new project excites me. I'll make it worth every heart-pounding, adrenaline racing, panty-melting moment we have together.

Bringing up her profile again, I comb over her list of hard and soft limits until I memorize them. She seems mostly open to everything I love. That's refreshing.

Man, her picture is adorable. Big hazel eyes peer out of a curtain of dark wavy hair. Her mouth is sexy as hell. My dick hardens thinking about the things I want to do to it.

Christ, I need a release.

My hand has been my only companion for a while, and it's not enough anymore. Growling, I head into my bedroom and pull out a few extra accessories to hopefully help me get off. The fact that her photo has keyed up my lust like this is unheard of. I work with beautiful people on a daily basis and never get hard like this. Tonight, one selfie of a woman I don't know has me undone.

What kind of sorcery is that?

I stare at her profile and pull out my stainless-steel urethral rod. Most men use it to get hard. I use it to enhance the pleasure points I discovered inside my cock. Pushing the tip inside, I start slow, nearly fucking my own cock with the long, skinny, textured rod. Holding the ring at the end, I ease it in and out of my dick, my eyes rolling back with ecstasy. Fuuuck, it's like finally scratching an itch you never could reach before.

Pulling the rod out, I lube up and slide my hand over my shaft, gripping it painfully hard. Then I snag my cell and stare at her picture again as I plan my first scene...

"Run, little mouse."

She dashes across the lawn, her hair flying behind her. Soon, I'll have all that dark hair wrapped around my fist.

I close my eyes, relishing the sound of her feet pounding across the yard as she picks up speed to get away from me. A smile tugs at my lips. Prowling in the direction I hear her go, I take my time and let her think she's managed to put enough distance between us.

She hasn't, but I'll pretend.

She'll think she's safe. She isn't, but I'll pretend.

She'll think she can outrun me. She won't, but I'll pretend.

Cold air puffs out of my mouth. My long strides quickly bring me closer to the border of the woods. A twig snaps in the distance and I turn my head in that direction. Slowing my breathing, I close my eyes and listen closely again.

I catch faint rasps as air saws out of her lungs. Poor thing, she's already out of breath and the chase has only begun.

"Little Mouse."

I sense movement to my right and the distinct crunch of leaves. I almost shoot off in that direction but realize it's a squirrel. I lick my lips and stalk forward, zeroing in on the sound of her frantic breaths again. My nostrils flare, desperate to smell her cunt.

She takes off to my left and I beat feet to catch up with her. Instead of tackling her to the ground, I circle around and head her off at the pass. Gasping, she stops in her tracks, her hazel eyes blowing wide in surprise that I beat her.

She backs up.

"You can't outrun me." With a deep growl, I lunge forward and wrap my arms around her torso,

then kick her legs out. She crumbles like a fawn on shaky legs. I let go, hoping she'll try to get away from me again.

Pricurious twists around and crawls out from under my body. I let her think she's escaped.

Then I snag her foot and drag her back where she belongs — under me. Pining her down, I bite the flesh on her shoulder to make her yell out. As she kicks and claws at the dirt ground, I yank her pants down, and —

Come so hard, my voice cracks with the roar I make.

Holy hell, I didn't even get to the best part of my fantasy and my body's response is to explode. Fuck. Me. What a head rush. Staring at the cum all over my stomach, I swipe my hand across it, smearing it all over my heated skin.

I hope Pricurious lives up to my fantasies.

But more importantly, I hope I live up to hers.

Chapter 4

Mak

I show up at the boudoir studio a little early and have second guessed every outfit I've brought with me since the moment I left my damn apartment. My goal is to make the most of out of this session, so not only have I packed a couple of sexy, lacy lingerie outfits, but I also brought props. Except now I feel stupid for bringing any of it because what the actual fuck am I doing?

With a death grip on the straps of my overstuffed bookbag, I take the elevator up to the fourth floor. My heart is pounding. My palms are all sweaty and gross. This is nutty. I don't know why I'm so nervous.

Oh, who am I kidding? Yes, I do. I'm scared I'll be judged for what I've brought. And that I'll look dumb in my outfits. This could easily turn out to be a huge waste of money and time, which will suck donkey balls since I don't have much of either, and wasting any of it on this session makes me feel woozy.

Ding!

The elevator stops and the doors slide open. Okay. I made it. I'm here.

I refuse to turn back now.

A huge, whitewashed brick wall directly across from me is graffitied all over with the words *Cruz Photography* spray painted in a vibrant yellow. There's only one way to go from here, and that's through those double glass doors beckoning me on the right.

Rolling my shoulders back, I suck in a deep breath and blow it all out.

Confidence is key.

Goddess-level awesomeness, here I come.

Pushing the glass doors open, the scent of this space hits me first, which throws me off. I don't know what I was expecting, but lavender's not it. Gorgeous, framed photos and canvas prints line the walls around the reception area that's lined with black leather chairs. Holy shit, these photos are S-E-X-Y. All body types, clothing styles, and poses—and not a single one looks awful.

This gives me hope.

When I made this appointment a while back, I'd barely looked through the website. Cruz Photography came highly recommended and was local, which was good enough for me. I didn't really think much about it other than I knew my boyfriend would be psyched to get steamy pics of me as a present.

Now I'm here for myself and my entire

plan has shifted.

Along the back of the reception desk is a line of photography awards. Jeez, this guy really must be good to have all that. It would explain the price of this session.

A perky, blue-haired woman about four inches taller than me waves from behind the desk. "Hi, I'm Chloe. Are you Makayla?"

At five-foot one inch, I grab her hand and shake it like I'm really a six-foot-seven linebacker. "Just Mak."

"It's nice to meet you, Mak. Carson's setting up right now, so you can come with me, and I'll get your makeup and hair going."

I follow her into a salon style room that has a ton of hair products and makeup stacked all over the place. It looks like a cosmetic warehouse exploded in here. The back of the room is lined with a ton of outfits on racks, along with shoes, crowns, and robes. There's a box of panty liners, and even boob tape.

My gaze lands on a set of huge black wings hanging on a mount. "Whoa."

Chloe stands next to me and admires them too. "Gorgeous, aren't they?"

"Yeah."

"Took me over seventy hours to make them. It was a labor of love and sheer stubbornness."

I gawk at her. "You *made* them? That's incredible."

"I love making cosplay stuff. Carson saw these and had to have them in here for his clients. No one has used them, which sucks." She runs her hands over the big feathers. "They look spectacular."

I have no doubt.

"So…" She claps her hands and rubs her palms together. "I've read over your form, and I see you're going for simple sultry."

That's one way to put it. "Yeah. I wasn't really sure what look I was going for when I filled that out. Figured simple was best. I have a bunch of outfits with me, because I wasn't sure which ones I would want to wear."

"I get that. Better to bring too many and be prepared for anything than have regrets because you held back."

She gets me. "Exactly." My smile falls. "But I broke up with my boyfriend months ago, so my original plan is out the window. I called to cancel yesterday but got talked into keeping my slot." That's kind of true. Not that the photographer had to say much to sway me. "I want to use these photos to maybe help boost my Instagram account. Well, not all the pics, because they'd probably get me banned, but some of them." I shut up before I prattle off too much and bore her to death.

Chloe taps the back of a swivel chair for me to sit in. Once I drop into it, she spins me to face the mirror. "Your hair is stunning, Mak."

"Thanks." It's so thick and heavy, I have an undercut to prevent headaches.

"I'm thinking…" Chloe fans my hair out across my shoulders and tips her head. "Soft waves?"

"Sounds good." I hope she can manage it. "My hair doesn't really hold a curl for long."

"Ohhh, challenge accepted." She grabs a can of some kind of hair product I don't recognize and sprays it in the air. "Watch me work my magic."

A half hour later, I'm in full makeup, my hair is done, and I'm in the changing room putting on my first outfit. Chloe talked her ass off the entire time. I'm sure she thought it was helpful, but I couldn't turn my head off long enough for anything she said to penetrate. She definitely drinks a lot of caffeine if these empty coffee cups are any indication. I swear she talks more than me too. That's saying something.

Rock music pumps through the speakers in the main room and I hear a man's voice say, "Mak ready, Chloe?"

"Yeah, she'll be out in a few minutes. Hey, I'm going to grab a latte down the road. You want anything?"

"I'll take a smoothie," he says.

"You're so weird. Who would choose a smoothie over a triple mocha frap with extra whipped cream and cinnamon?"

I snicker from behind the changing room

door, listening to them.

"Why would someone want a heart attack in a cup when they can have joy in a cup instead?"

"I guess that means you want the avocado one with coconut?"

"It's like you can read my mind, Chloe."

"Or you just never get anything but that. You're so boring, man. Switch things up a bit. Be adventurous. Try the watermelon cactus flower smoothie or something."

"Maybe next time. Hey, see if Mak wants anything too, will ya? Tell her it's my treat."

"No prob, boss."

I back away from the door and smooth out the first of several outfits I've brought. I know I won't wear some of them, but this one was my most scandalous, and I love how I look in it. It's a black lacey number with a matching see-through robe that fits more like a cardigan. I feel like a million dollars in it.

Until I look in the mirror.

Holy crap. What am I thinking going out in this? "Pull yourself together, Mak. You look great."

If I keep saying it to myself, maybe it'll sink in. Besides, I'm paying Cruz Photography a small fortune, so hopefully he has fancy editing software that will make me look like the Mak that lives in my head. I'll just have to double check to make sure the photographer understands my expectations before I leave.

"Mak?" Chloe softly knocks. "You need me to lace, tie, zip or pin anything?"

"Nope." I blow out a big breath and swing the door open. "I'm as good as I'm gonna get, I think."

Chloe's eyes widen and her mouth drops. "DAYEM GIRL! You are *fine*!"

I appreciate the hype more than she'll ever know.

"Listen, I'm off to grab some more nectar of the gods. You want anything? Latte, frap, gross healthy smoothie?"

"I'm good, but thanks." I can't imagine eating or drinking anything right now. My stomach is in knots.

"Okay, well there's water and fruit in the fridge. If you change your mind in the next forty-five minutes, just have Carson text me and I'll bring you something. No worries."

"Sounds good. Thanks." Stepping out, I hang a left and the rest of the studio comes into view. Holy shit, it's massive. Props and different scenes are set up all over the place. They're set up for everything in here. Literally. Everything.

There's even a tub.

My gaze drifts over to a gilded bird cage big enough for a full-grown person to stand in. Then my eyes sail back to the tub with the chandelier hanging above it. There's also a bed with a dark grey headboard, a sex swing hanging between a leather couch and a fireplace. OMG, they even have an old 50's style bar that's perfect for a pinup girl to sit on, complete with black and chrome stools.

Several props hang from rolling carts out here too. And lighting. So much lighting and filters.

"Hi Mak, I'm Carson."

Turning around, I freeze. Tall, dark, and hot as sin, Carson makes his way across the room, holding a camera.

Holy. Shit.

No.

No, no, no, no.

There's no way this guy is who I think it is. Carson's rich brown eyes bore into mine as he stands there with his hand out for me to shake.

Play it cool, Mak. Don't make this any more awkward than it already is. "Nice to meet you..." *WolfByte.*

Before I say another word, he lets go of my hand and steps back. "Ready?"

"Yup." Maybe I'm losing my mind. My warped imagination probably jumped to WolfByte only because I stayed up all night staring at that man's profile pic. Okay, I've *definitely* spent too much time online if I'm this flustered over a possible encounter with someone I may be contemplating signing a sex contract with.

If he *is* WolfByte, and he recognizes me,

wouldn't he say something? Maybe not. I mean, I'm not saying anything either, so this could all be nothing. Besides, WolfByte has those two piercings on his lips and this guy doesn't. Wait, does he? There are no hoops in his bottom lip, but it looks like he has two holes. Or am I imagining things?

Shit, now I'm staring too long at his mouth.

I can't seem to stop.

Lift your gaze, idiot! Lift. Your. Gaze.

"Let's get started." Carson flashes a smile before turning away from me.

Goddamn he has a nice ass.

"We can start over at the bed if you'd like." He holds up a paper and reads over it.

I assume it's the form I filled out when I first reserved this session. "I don't really want the bed." I cringe a little. "I'd like something more… unconventional, I think. I'm sorry. I should have asked to fill out a new form yesterday, but I completely forgot about the questionnaire I'd submitted to you before."

He's going to kick me out for being a pain in the ass, and I don't blame him.

Instead, Carson folds the paper up and shoves it into his back pocket. "No problem at all." He seems completely unfazed that what he's prepared for may no longer be what I want. "Do you have anything specific in mind?"

"No. I was hoping you could maybe take some creative liberties."

His smile reminds me of what a villain's might be like. Hungry and sexy. "Good thing Chloe stretched you out for this."

"Excuse me?"

His mouth turns down in a frown. "She didn't stretch you?"

"Ummm. No?" I play with the hem of my robe, and somehow manage to completely forget I'm wearing next to nothing, standing in front of a hot man holding a camera. "Should she have?"

"Yes." He lets out a grumbling sigh. "Holding poses can cause muscle cramps and soreness."

"Jeez. You bend your clients like pretzels or something?"

"Sometimes."

I don't miss the playfulness in his tone. I also don't miss the way my heart beats faster.

"Hang on a sec." He dashes into the room Chloe did my hair and makeup in and comes out with two rolled up yoga mats. While I gawk at his ass, Carson lays out the mats and kicks his shoes off.

What is happening here?

He sits on his mat and pats the one next to him that's staggered with his. "I promise it's worth it."

I'm barefoot in a skimpy lingerie outfit and we're about to do yoga stretches. *Okay, Mak. Be chill.* I still can't tell if this is WolfByte or not, but I promised myself before I arrived that I wasn't going to hold myself back or be insecure or get too up in my head and talk myself out of something while I'm here.

This isn't a big deal unless I make it one.

Plopping down on my mat, I wait for his instruction.

"Good girl."

Fuck. Me.

"Put your legs out in front of you. Flex and point your feet for a count of twenty."

I swear I'm thrown back to my old yoga sessions with my best friend, Leah. It feels good to stretch and now I can't remember why we quit yoga in the first place. Before long, more of the tension that keeps building in my body loosens and I'm more comfortable. The lavender in the air helps too.

This is lovely.

"Reach out as far as you comfortably can towards your toes."

Smiling, my muscle memory kicks in, and my spine straightens; then I lift my arms up and bend over until I'm halfway to my feet. Hey, it's been a while, alright? My hammies are tight.

Carson, however, stretches all the way out and grips his damn ankles.

"You're bendy," I blurt out. Holy shit, why did I just say that out loud? Can't my thoughts just stay on the inside, for fuck's sake?

Instead of responding, he straightens back up and instructs me through five more different stretches for my arms and legs. When he has us go into child's pose, I almost groan with how good it feels in my lower back. I need to go back to yoga. This is so relaxing.

"Last one," he says, repositioning again. "Cat-cow." Carson gets on all fours and looks back at me. "Curl up, arching your back like a pissed off cat."

I do.

"Good. Now retract and curl your back as deep as you can. Stick your butt up and tilt your head back for me."

No problem.

I hold the pose, relishing how nice it feels on my back, and I swear he growls. I know it's probably my overactive imagination, but... I think he just growled again. It's low and rumbly and hot and —

Get. A. Grip.

I can't stop circling back to WolfByte, and as I do two more Cat-Cow stretches, I imagine what it would feel like to be fucked hard in this position. To hear him growl in my ear as he rails me. To feel his fingers dig into my thighs when he pries them apart to eat my pussy.

Heat blooms down my body and I feel myself getting wet. Oh no. No, no, no. I'm not in the right outfit for this nonsense. This is getting embarrassing.

"That's it," Carson says, standing up. "You should be all warmed up and ready for me now."

I'm ready alright. But it's not to have my stupid picture taken.

Sitting back on my legs, I recollect myself. "That felt so good."

"I'm glad." He holds out his hands for me to take and lifts me up to my feet effortlessly. Carson's a solid guy. He's one of those hotties with a dad bod, but is still super muscular. He seems like the kind of guy who works out a lot but also loves beer and nachos.

That's my type.

His hands are huge, as is the rest of him. I like every inch I see. My mind immediately paints a scenario where he picks me up and cups my ass with those big hands of his and rails me against the wall. Bet his thrusts would be deep and hard. Bet he could rearrange my organs and make me call him Sir.

Lust pools in my pussy and my hands grow clammy.

Carson inhales sharply and my cheeks flame because I'm scared he can sense how turned on I am. But that's ridiculous, right? He can't smell it. That's… no. I quickly let go of his hands and back away.

Come on, Mak. Pull yourself together! So what if I'm turned on? Anyone would be with a man like this staring down at them. What is he? Six-three? Six-four?

His nostrils flare and eyes darken.

Fuck. There's no way in hell he can smell how turned on I am, right? I'm just being paranoid. That sort of thing only happens in spicy books and I'm not living in one of those.

That would be so cool, though.

Carson turns away from me again and starts rolling up our yoga mats. "What kind of music would you like?"

"I ummmm. I don't care."

"Come on, Makayla," he says in a cute, teasing way. "There has to be a band you enjoy. What's your favorite genre? I'll put it on, and we can get started."

"I…" Biting my lip, I reclaim my fluttering heart and focus. "I've been on a K-pop kick lately."

My ex, Dick-twat-who-shall-not-be-named, always gave me shit for liking certain genres, and it drove me nuts. To the point where I only played music in the car by myself or in earbuds when I soaked in a bath, because he never even let me listen to my amazing playlists on the surround system that he insisted on getting me for Christmas two years ago. No, no, that was reserved for *his* music most of the time. And *his* movies. And *his* video games.

Blackpink starts up and I swear my heart swoons from the grin Carson gives me. Then he arches his brow and says, "Creative liberties, right?"

I clear my throat. "Yeah. Create away. I'm

all yours."

Carson tips his chin towards the sex swing. "Lean against that wall right there, with your back to me, and spread your legs."

Chapter 5

Carson

This woman might be the death of me. No, not might. She *will* be the death of me.

Stretching her just now nearly had me growling with need, and my professionalism almost slipped. Her obedience is delicious when she does everything I tell her to. *Such a good girl.* Don't get me going on the way her hips sway as she walks over to the wall and gets into position.

But the kill shot?

Her eyes. This woman's hazel eyes would have started whole ass wars back in the day. She's angelic and demonic all in one breath.

And my dick is hardening. *Shit.*

"Like this?" Mak leans against the wall behind the sex swing.

I clear my throat and get my head back in the game. "Yeah." Gripping my camera, I slowly prowl closer to her. "Rest your elbows against the brick and put your hands into your hair."

She fidgets a little, as if unsure about what I want. "Like this?"

Not quite. "May I touch you?"

"Yeah, sure. Just reconfigure me however I'm supposed to be."

I don't want to just reconfigure her. I want to fuck her brains out against the wall.

Placing my boots on either side of her feet, I grab her hips and pull them out towards my groin. "Bend this one for me," I say, tapping her right leg. "And relax your shoulders and roll them back. Good. Now stay just like that."

I back away and start snapping pics. Christ, her ass is phenomenal. I want to bite those cheeks and leave teeth marks on them.

"Okay, now come back to where I'm standing."

Mak locks gazes with me, waiting for more instruction as she comes closer.

I snap pictures of it without looking through the lens. Fuck me, she's spectacular at every angle.

"Let your robe fall off your shoulders and put your arms out a little, like this." I show her exactly what I want, and she mimics me. "Nice. Now lift onto your tiptoes and walk towards that big window over there, crossing your footsteps as you go."

She starts moving away from me and stumbles. "Shit. Wait. Let me restart."

I bite back my smile. I'm not laughing that she faltered. I'm pleased she's willing to try again until she's comfortable with it. I snap pictures constantly, even when she restarts two more times before making it all the way to the window.

Mak looks over her shoulder at me again. "How was that?"

Click. I take another pic of her. "Perfection."

She huffs a little like she doesn't believe me.

I don't lie. I can already tell these photos are going to be some of my best work and I'm willing to bet I'll barely touch up a fucking thing during edits. After taking Mak through several more poses, I finally get to readjust my rock-hard dick when she does a wardrobe change.

"Ready!" she says, beaming a smile at me from the changing room doorway.

Holyyyyy fffffuuuuucccckkk.

Lace and leather are always nice but give me a woman in an oversized sweater and nothing underneath any day of the week.

Mak's sweater hangs off one shoulder and is just long enough to hug and hide the phenomenal flare of her ass that I've already seen and can't stop drooling over. I want to pluck a thread and unravel it, just to reveal her gorgeous body a little at a time.

"I've changed my mind." She tucks her hair behind her ear. "Can we maybe do a couple photos on the bed?"

"Absolutely." I rush to set up lighting and filters because the sunlight has already changed.

After a few test shots and readjustments, I pat the mattress. "Crawl on up."

"Shit. I forgot something. Hang on!" She rushes back to the changing room and returns to me with a stack of books in her arms. I cock my eyebrow, but she doesn't see it. Mak's too busy picking out what, I presume, is her favorite story, and climbs up on the bed with it. "I want to be a sexy bookworm."

That's my type…

Clearing my suddenly dry throat, I grab a bottle of water and chug some of it before getting back to business. "Sit in the center, legs crossed, but with one knee up."

"Like this?"

Exactly. I snap a pic. "Drape your sweater a little lower on your shoulder." Her neck is perfect for biting. Fuck, I want to lick her collarbone so bad. "Good. Chin up." I want to suck on that throbbing vein in her neck. "Roll your shoulders back and lift the book to your face." I barely recognize the cover at first, but then it clicks. "You like shifter smut?"

"Love it."

Good to know. I continue taking pictures of her in every spicy pose I can think of with her book until Mak makes her way off the bed and onto the floor.

She gazes up at me with all her books surrounding her. "I feel like a sexy Belle from Beauty and the Beast."

I agree. "Living a spicier provincial life, huh?"

"Totally." She arches her back, posing on her own. I snap more pictures, loving how relaxed and comfortable she's become around me. "Was that your favorite princess movie?"

"No. It's too traumatizing."

I lower my camera. "How so?"

"The moment the Beast's curse breaks and he turns human again has to be one of the greatest let downs in cinematic history."

I burst out laughing. "He wasn't *that* bad."

"Then you can have him. I'm a Beast girl, now and forever."

Be still my caged heart.

"I think we're good with these. Want to do another wardrobe change?"

"Yes, please."

To my surprise, she lifts the sweater over her head, revealing a tank top that says, "My favorite color is morally grey" with a set of fangs on it. Paired with black panties, this woman looks positively sinful. I need to reel in my focus and regain some professionalism here. I've never faltered like this before and it's starting to unnerve me.

"So, how long have you been a photographer?"

"Since middle school."

Her eyes widen with surprise. "Really?"

"Yeah. I'm not a people person, but

FOMO's a bitch. Holding a camera solved the issue. I was in the mix, but not. Happy I went out, but relieved that most people left me the fuck alone."

Her silence causes me to look up from my camera. Did I say something wrong? Wouldn't be the first time, or the millionth, but I'd like to know if I have.

"That's..." Her mouth curves into a lopsided smile. "Really relatable, actually."

"You into photography too?"

"Hell no, I don't know the first thing about fancy cameras. But I'm socially awkward and hate crowds. Hence, the books." She fans the pages of the paperback in her hand.

"Take one with you everywhere you go, huh?"

"I'd feel naked without one. I even have spares in my car, another in my purse, and an app on my phone for emergency purposes."

"Does that mean you went to parties and sat in the corner to read by yourself?"

"You better believe it. I'm not into drinking, or anything that alters my mind, even temporarily. All my friends were huge partiers, and I came from a small town in the middle of nowhere, so if you weren't drunk in a cornfield on a Friday night, you were high in someone's barn pretending it was a rave." She rolls her eyes. "I also didn't want to feel left out, so I'd go, but never actually immersed in any of it. I'm better now, but not by much."

I realize I've dropped my camera to my thigh and have stalked closer to her. Giving Mak my full attention comes naturally, and I'm not about to break whatever connection this is becoming. "At least you're doing what you love."

"True." She tips her head, reminding me of a fox studying her newest meal. "What got you into boudoir photography?"

Swallowing, I grip my camera tighter and debate on how much to say. Part of me wants to say a lot of things that I don't normally share, which throws me off my game a bit. Erring on the side of caution, I go with my usual explanation. And yet, because the universe hates me, the first thing that flies out of my mouth is *not* what I intended. "I was bullied a lot for being overweight as a kid." I tap my gut. "No matter how much I work out, I'll never get rid of this extra cushion. I'm a natural big boy."

Mak's hands fall into her lap as she continues staring at me.

I keep talking, like a dumbass, but skirt past the whole truth and tell her a secondary one instead. "Anyway, I know self-image can be important. I was dating this one girl back in college who had a lot of insecurities. I thought she was stunning, and she couldn't see what I saw when she looked in the mirror. No amount of compliments I gave her worked. Nothing I did in the bedroom convinced her, either. So, I started taking her picture."

My chest constricts. I need to shut up, but I don't.

"My camera doesn't judge or define a person. It celebrates them in a way most people don't get to see often. It can capture their beauty when they least expect it. I took photos of her, which she was hesitant about at first, until she saw the results." I'll never forget that day. "The look on her face is burned in my mind forever. She saw what my camera captured, without a single bit of photoshopping or editing, and she fell in love with herself for the first time. That's when I knew boudoir photography was going to be my thing. Every client that walks through my door will eventually have the same look on their face as my first girlfriend did."

Mak's eyes grow watery, and that makes me feel weird, so I quickly recover and get back to business. "Okay, enough bullshitting. Hook your thumb under your strap." She immediately obeys me again. "Good girl. Now lift your other arm up and bring your hand up into your hair. Elbow in. Now soften your fingers in your hair."

"Like…" Her voice cracks a little. "This?"

"Perfect." I snap a dozen more pics and then lower my camera again. The fire burning in my sternum dies down because we're back to safe conversation. Mak didn't circle back to my past, and I'm sure as shit not going to either.

"You're incredibly easy to photograph, Mak. You're making my job too easy."

She bursts out in laughter and the tension, or whatever it is growing between us, pops like a bubble. "Careful. You might have spoken too soon. I have one more outfit to get on, if there's still time."

Her tone lifts at the end as if she's asking a question… or for permission. "Fuck yeah. Let's do it."

I don't even bother looking at the clock to see what time it is. My other client can wait. Rude, I know, but I'm enjoying myself and don't want to rush Mak out of here. Besides, Chloe is back from her hour-long coffee break and she's great at reading the room. She'll distract my other client if I run over on time.

Mak dashes into the changing room again and I hold my breath, anxious to see what she comes out in next. It takes her much longer than I expect, but when I hear Chloe laugh and say something that makes her crack up, the unease in my chest lifts a little.

"Okay…" Mak comes out of the room. "How can we make this look cool in a pic?"

I freeze, enthralled. Mak just came out in the set of motherfucking black wings.

I swear a new kink unlocks in me.

Something hits my boot and I barely notice it until Mak's eyes get huge and she rushes over to me. "Your camera!"

"What?" I snap out of my stupor. "Oh shit." I'd dropped my fucking camera.

Mak holds it like it's a baby bird that just fell out of its nest. If this thing isn't broken, it'll be a miracle. My palms sweat and heart races as I pluck it out of her tiny hands and hit a few buttons. *Oh, thank fuck.* "It's good."

"Phew." She sags in relief.

I snap a few pics just to make sure, but yeah, everything's in working order. My brain immediately starts rapid firing different backdrops and poses to put Mak in to showcase this outfit. I love the wings Chloe designed, but no one's ever used them before, which is a shame.

If I believed in fate, I'd say they were made and waiting for Mak to put them on.

"Hang tight." I know exactly what we need, I just hope I can reach it with all the junk I've got stored in my closet.

Pushing the door open, I climb over stools, baskets, candelabras, and a bunch of other props to reach the back left corner. Shit, I really need to straighten shit up in here. Oh hey, there's that box fan I was looking for last week.

Nearly toppling over a stack of cushions and a tub of silk sheets, I finally reach the backgrounds rolled up in the back. Plucking out the dark grey one, I also grab a shag carpet. Tripping and climbing, the struggle to get it out of here is real, but I make it out alive.

"Shit. I forgot the candles." Propping the screen up first, I go back in and fight my way through the treacherous obstacle course and dig out a box of candelabras and glitter I had left over from a convention a few years back. "Okay. Give me a sec."

I get busy setting up a new scene and am acutely aware that Mak's watching my every move. I have the urge to speak and fill the silence, but I bite the inside of my cheek and focus on getting everything ready for her instead. I just hope she likes my vision for this, or I'm going to feel like such a loser.

"Okay," I say, wiping my brow. "This should do it." I look over at Mak and offer her a smile. She gawks at me like I'm the one who just sprouted wings.

"This is amazing," she says, breathlessly. When Mak storms past me to see the details I've managed to scrape together, I get the opportunity to appreciate her outfit from the back.

Yup. This woman is here to ruin me.

Her ass is absolute perfection.

Just like the rest of her.

We take a bunch of pictures and she's the one who hears my next client come in first. There's no way they can see us—not with how I designed my space—but it's clear to me by Mak's body language that she's uncomfortable that someone else is here.

Probably because the only thing covering her tits right now are her hands.

"Any more outfits?"

"No," she says, quietly.

"Okay. You can get changed, and I'll let you have a peek at a few of these when you come back out."

"Um. Okay."

She's clearly uncomfortable now, and it's not being in this room, topless, with me. I'll do whatever it takes to ease her worries. "No one is in the dressing room," I assure her, in case that's the reason she's being weird. "My next client will stay out in the waiting area until I give Chloe the green light."

That seems to relieve her considerably.

"Okay." Mak leaves and I'm still admiring her ass until she slips out of my sight. Cleaning up the scene, I roll up the carpet and collapse the backdrop.

Mak comes out with her overstuffed book bag on her shoulders and I'm not lying when I say this might be her sexiest outfit yet. Jeans and a hoodie, messy bun and Chucks.

My dick can't handle that combo.

I'm so hard it hurts.

Eager for a distraction, I crook my thumb at her, silently beckoning Mak to come closer. Clicking through the pics, I find a few random good ones to show her. "Take a look."

"No," she says. "I'm good. I'd rather just be

surprised by the gallery you email me later."

Oooookay. "Here." I put my camera down and stretch my hand out towards her. "Let me carry your bag for you and walk you to your car."

"Oh no, that's not necessary."

"I insist. It looks heavy."

She chews on her lip and slips it off her dainty shoulders. It lands with a thud on the floor. I pick it up, struck by how heavy it truly is, and chuckle. "Jesus. Did you bring your entire book collection or what?"

"Not even close," she says. "I'd need a U-Haul for that."

Damn, Mak isn't a very big woman, yet she made this heavy ass bag seem light when she carried it. For some reason, that turns me on too. She's strong. Bet she's hella fun to play with in bed…

My dick twitches.

Holy hell, everything about her keeps igniting my flames. I'm kind of grateful her session is over because I'm not sure how much longer I would have lasted.

"Let's get this sack of bricks to your car."

"No, no, you have another client. I can't possibly hold you up any longer than I already have."

Chloe laughs from the dressing room and my next client says something about big dick energy. I wish I didn't have another photo session today. I want to walk Mak to her car. Scratch that, I want to take her home with me and do despicably dirty things to her body.

My heart's racing again, and I hate the reason for it. My professionalism has blown out the damn window today and there's only one reason why.

Mak caught me off guard coming here, looking like this, smelling this way, sounding like that.

Fffffuuuuuccccckkkk.

I'm not ready to unleash her yet. "Let me at least get you as far as the elevator."

"Okay," she says, smiling as we head out to the main area together. "This was fun. I'm glad I came." She takes the bag from me as she steps into the elevator.

"I'm glad you came too." I'd love to make her come in other ways, too.

"Well." Mak blows out a shaky exhale. "Bye, Carson."

The door starts slowly closing, and I seize the moment. A low growl rumbles out of the back of my throat, and I love that her breath hitches hearing it. "Talk soon, *Pricurious*."

Her eyes go wide with shock just as the door shuts.

Chapter 6

Mak

I knew it. I fucking knew it! Carson *is* WolfByte and now I'm seething mad. He knew this whole time that it was me and didn't say jackshit about it. Of course, neither did I, but that's because I had my doubts and second guessed myself. He just looked me deadass in the eye and called me by my kink app name.

Carson didn't second-guess shit. Confident, and probably loving that I was basically clueless that it really was him, he waited until the end of our session to throw that bomb at me.

Holy shit, I'm soooo embarrassed. It was bad enough that I dressed in all that lingerie in front of a stranger to take photos of me, but then I got topless and put on those damn wings—because he was seriously making me feel so great in there and I wanted to be adventurous and spicy—and I really let my bookworm flag fly.

Then he walks me to the elevator like a gentleman, only to leave me gaping with my mouth on the floor as the door shuts and cuts off any words I might have come up with had my mind not just been blown.

Well played, Carson. Well. Fucking. Played.

Holy shit, my head's spinning. We connected so well. Like, we immediately clicked. Why didn't he tell me it was him all along? Was he trying to remain professional? Maybe. I mean, I would if it were me. Being in a Dom/sub relationship should come with some discretion and I haven't signed the contract yet anyways, so why jump the gun, right?

Damn. That man could be chasing me through the woods and fucking me?

Be still my quivering pussy.

Ding! The door opens and I head out of the building, gripping the straps to my bookbag, while simultaneously trying to gather my wits. I'm so confused on how to feel about this now.

Cool air hits my face and I'm grateful winter is almost here. I'm so hot and bothered… no, I mean hot and pissed off… I grumble a million incoherent words as I head to my car.

Bet he didn't say anything because he's not into me.

I bet it was the K-pop. Or the smut books.

Or my hair and figure.

Oh no, did I have something in my teeth?

I was so determined to be myself and not hold back thinking I was never going to see this photographer again so it wouldn't matter and… and we shared such personal things—especially on his end—fuck, now he's probably going to rescind the contract and block my ass online.

How did I let my guard down like that?

How did I once again second guess that it was WolfByte? I should have gone with my initial instincts and just asked him. I could have brought up the app in a nonchalant way. I could have paid better attention to his mouth and noticed if there were piercing holes from his snake bites. But nooooo. What was I doing? Spending a tremendous amount of energy keeping my lust in check and bouncing between turned on and easy-going because Carson made that session so fun and stress-free. It was natural to pose, even if some of the positions were hard to hold. And if I wasn't focused on doing what he told me, I was busy sneaking peeks at his fantastic ass, sinewy forearms, and broad back.

Carson's my type.

I love a man with meat on his bones. The dad bod thing he's rocking is totally up my alley. Fuuuck. I'm starting to sweat. Aren't I too young for a hot flash? Shit.

Carson's hot and fun and big and talented—he's the total package.

And can we just talk about how easy Carson is to be around? I mean, hell, I just did yoga in lacey underwear with him and didn't feel embarrassed at all.

Holy fuckballs. Carson is WolfByte.

His profile picture has longer hair and lip piercings—both of which are major turn-ons for me—but now that I've seen him in person, the only thing that's changed is my desire. It's so much higher now.

I can't believe he didn't say something about me being Pricurious sooner. I feel steamrolled by emotions I refuse to grasp. Shit, I need to think this through. Fuck that, I need to phone a friend.

Dropping my bag in the backseat of my car, I rummage for my phone and quickly dial my best friend, Leah. She picks up on the second ring.

"Hey."

"Hey," I sigh, sitting in my car with my head tipped back. "I need to overthink something out loud."

"Oh goodie. Let me get comfy first." Muffled noises fill my ears and then she says, "Okay, I'm ready. Go."

"Well… I joined that kink app."

"Nice!"

"Yeah. Until the Dom who sent me a contract last night happens to also be my boudoir photographer today."

Leah busts out laughing. "You have the *worst* fucking luck, Mak! What happened? Did you bang all over his studio and never bother with the pics?"

"No," I grumble. "He didn't mention it at all."

"Maybe he didn't recognize you."

"Oh, he did. And I'm pissed because he waited to the last minute as I was out the door to mention it."

"Oh. My. God."

"And the second I saw him, I thought I recognized him, but I didn't say anything about it because I wasn't sure. I feel dumb now."

"Well maybe he likes keeping his career and private life separate, Mak."

That makes sense, but it raises another question. "Then why bring it up at all?"

"Because maybe he doesn't want you blindsided after you sign that contract and see him again. That would definitely freak me out."

That's what I'm thinking too. Some of my embarrassment and anger fizzles out.

"So…" I can practically hear Leah waggling her eyebrows on the other end of the line. "Is he hot?"

"Yes." I pinch the bridge of my nose. "And he's exactly my type."

"Ohhh sweet!"

"Ugh. I totally nerded out with him today too."

"Bet he's a sucker for a bookworm. Aw, just imagine it. You, reading your book, him, willing to reenact the scenes. This is the best thing ever!"

That does sound incredible. And very far-fetched.

Leah squeals in my ear. "He's big, primal, and can make all your kinky wishes come true and *then* photo document it for his spank bank keepsakes."

"Not funny, Leah."

"I'm not laughing!" Yes, she is. "I'm still not seeing what the problem is here."

"I put on these huge wings and went topless!" I yell. Leah goes silent for a moment and all I hear is my heart swishing in my ears.

"Good. For. You. Mak."

I want to die.

"You're going to fuck him anyway. He's going to see your body no matter what, right? You basically just gave him a peek of what he's going to get later. Girrrl, I bet he got so hard looking at you."

My face heats again. "You're not really helping."

"Hey, I'd get hard for you if I had a dick. You're like a compact ball of fuckable fun."

"Stop."

"Seriously. A pocket-sized spicy bookworm."

"Knock it off."

"You're a spinner. Do you know how many men want a tiny woman they can impale and..." She makes a whizzing sound. "Zzzzzzzzzz."

"I hate you."

"You love me." Leah sighs. "I'm really proud of you. You got out of your shell today."

Only because Carson made it easy.

"Lucky whore. Now you've got a hot Dom photographer probably foaming at the mouth for you to sign that contract and he's already dying to chase you."

"Stop."

"In the woods."

"Staahhhhp."

"Where he'll tackle you on the dirty leaf-covered ground and growl in your ear all the dirty things that'll make you drenched and begging for his big, shifter-sized dick."

"Hanging up now."

"Fuck me, Daddy."

"Nope."

"Fuck me, Wolfy."

"Someone make it stop."

"That's it, take me, you growly, sexy beast!"

"You're no longer my best friend." I can't stop laughing. "And it's WolfByte, by the way. B-Y-T-E." Shit, am I allowed to share that outside of the K!nkLink app? Fuck it. I tell Leah everything. Always.

"You're joking," she squeals. "He's a fucking nerd! A big, hot, tech nerd!"

I think she might be right, and yeah, that's a turn-on too. Carson is checking all my boxes and I'm super nervous about it. This all feels a little too good to be true. Glancing up at the windows on the fourth floor of the building, I bite my bottom lip and hope for the best because now I really want this to work out. Any anger I felt for him waiting until the last minute to call me by my profile name has melted into something lusty and eager.

"Okay, all jokes aside. What was his reaction to the wings and topless Mak?"

Leah's question catches me off guard. "Huh?"

"You wanted to overthink this, sooooo what was his reaction to the topless wing poses?"

Carson's pupils had blown wide and then he'd busted his ass to get stuff out of a storage room to set me up with a gorgeous backdrop. "He nearly broke his neck climbing through a closet to set up a scene just for me."

"Then he knows a good thing when he sees it and not only appreciates it but also brings it to the next level."

"That's a stretch."

"Don't let this opportunity slip by, Mak. Sign that contract and see where this goes."

I'd called her about the contract last night at two am when I was overthinking all the things. Leah was all in, of course, but I still wasn't sure and said I'd have to sleep on it. But when I woke up this morning, I was ready to make changes in my life. And I'm still ready, damnit. "You're right."

"Fuck yeah."

"I'm signing that contract."

"That's my girl!"

"I'm going to see where this goes."

"Arrrooooo!"

"You can stop that now."

"Never."

We start laughing again, and I feel ten times better. "Thanks for being there for me."

"Always, babe." She clanks dishes around in the background. "I'm just going to live vicariously through you until I meet my own Hotty MacHotterton who rocks my world."

"You can always join K!nkLink, you know."

"Mmm hmm." It sounds like she slams a cabinet shut. "Call me later, okay?"

"Yup." We hang up and before I drive out of the parking lot, I open the contract and skim over the details one last time before adding my signature. Tapping the submit button, I'm practically floating in my seat. Holy shit, I'm actually going to do this.

The prospect of Carson and me together, even for one night, has me lightheaded with anticipation. That growl he gave me at the elevator will live rent free in my head forever. Fuuuuck, I'm so ready to be the prey and get eaten by a big, sexy wolf like him.

Here's hoping that man really delivers as a Dom, and that I'm what he wants in a submissive.

Chapter 7

Carson

By the time I get home, I'm too tired to sleep and too wired to focus. Glitch, Ara, and Trey are probably online, since it's Tuesday night, but I'm not in the mood to kick their asses in a video game right now.

Ever since Mak left my studio, I've been unable to concentrate on a damned thing. It made my second session a challenge to get through. I shouldn't have called Mak out by saying her profile name when I did. That was a dick move.

But knowing who she was and not saying anything seemed even shittier.

She could have barged back into my studio and said something to me. She could have deleted the contract and never spoke another word to me. She could have done many things to let me know what I did was unacceptable. Instead, that sexy little woman chose to sign my contract.

She's mine to play with now.

It's almost too good to be true, and there's

a part of me that's still hesitant about all this. We clicked so well earlier today.

For someone who's about five feet tall and a hundred and twenty pounds soaking wet, she sure acts like a ten-foot-tall warrior goddess. Mak looked so comfortable and confident in her skin throughout most of the shoot, which was refreshing. All she needed was direction, which, goddamn did she take well each time.

I can't stop thinking about her. And fuuuck, that woman is beautifully made. Small up top, big on the bottom, lush thighs, thick hair, fat bottom lip, and big hazel eyes—the devil broke the mold with Mak.

And I'll gladly go to Hell for all the sinful things I'm dying to do to her.

Rummaging through my bag, I pull out the memory card and download both sessions from earlier today onto my computer. The instant I export the files and pull up the first one of Mak, my entire body hardens. Goddamn she's beautiful. Funny, she seemed more comfortable in front of my camera, half-naked in those wings, than she did completely covered in her bookworm outfit.

Holy fuck, look at her eyes.

Mak gazes at me from the screen. My dick hardens to the point of pain. Unzipping my pants, I pull my cock out and stroke it slowly. I shouldn't be doing this. It's not okay to jack off to your client's photos, and I've never in my life gone down this forbidden road before, but Mak isn't just a client.

As of five hours ago, she's also my play partner.

My heart pounded so hard when I got the notification saying she'd signed my contract. She's going to be very happy that she did. I'll make sure of it. The only reason I'm not calling her up so we can make arrangements right fucking now is because I want to give her time to back out. If I seem too eager, it might scare her off.

But I'm dying to get things started with that woman.

Spitting on my palm, I stroke myself while looking at picture after picture, after beautiful, stunning, mouth-wateringly sexy picture of my prey. My favorites are of her in the oversized sweater holding a shifter romance book. I almost told her that my friend, Trey, designed that particular book cover, but I didn't. Just like I also didn't tell her that I took the photo of the model on that cover.

It's serendipitous in a way, that she chose that book to pose with, but I didn't want to come off as a bragger.

Clicking through more of the shoot, I stop at one photo where Mak's posing with her back to the camera. Her black lace panties barely cover her luscious ass. She's gripping the bottom of her lace robe, her thighs smashed together,

her dainty little fingers curled around the hem. Mak's thick hair reaches the middle of her back, and I wanted nothing more than to pull that glorious mane while taking her from behind instead of standing several feet back, snapping her photos.

Holy shit, the way she posed, the scent I caught on her when we were stretching, the way her big doe eyes looked up at me from whatever pose I put her in…

"Ffffuuuuuuuuck." I beat off faster, harder, zeroing in on her pretty little mouth. I want to fuck it until her lips are swollen and red and drool drips off her chin. I want to come on her tongue and watch her spit it back out onto my cock.

"That's my good girl."

Squeezing my eyes shut, I grip my cock harder and jerk it faster. A growl erupts from between my clenched teeth. Thinking of her topless, with her tiny tits and big hips, those perfect little feet and her long hair, the way she kept watching me as I moved around her to take picture after picture, capturing every goddamn angle of her sweet perfection in those big black wings…

I blow my load in record time.

Shame takes hold of me, even as my heart's racing in my ribcage and dick's still throbbing in my palm. I shouldn't have done this. It's over-stepping a line. She didn't give consent to this and now I feel sick for using her pictures to find some relief for myself.

If I was a better man, I'd cancel the contract. If I was a more honorable gentleman, I wouldn't be gearing up to jack off again. My dick is still hard and sensitive, and I know full well I could chase a second release. I want another orgasm badly.

So, I deny myself as punishment.

"Fuck my life." After turning off my computer screen, I pull off my shirt and unbuckle my belt while climbing the steps to head to the bathroom. Hopefully a cold shower will help reset my body and mind.

Spoiler alert: It doesn't.

Fifteen minutes under the ice-cold spray and I'm still just as hard and needy as ever. Getting out of the house might help, because I can almost guarantee that staying here, with Mak's photos in need of editing, will not soothe my desperate need to fuck.

This requires a distraction. One bigger than I can get inside my house. Dressing in a hurry—as if the longer I stay in my house, the worse the temptation to work on Mak's photos will get—and I snag my keys and haul ass out my front door. There are only a few places I like in this town, but none of them will do for me now. I need something chaotic. Loud. With the new club that just opened up last month only a half hour away from me, why not try there?

Backing out of my driveway and ready to rock, I crank up the music as I tear through town to reach the other side of it.

"Shit." Once I pull into the lot, I can't even find a parking space. I end up in the back corner, which is dimly lit, and seriously start regretting my decision to come here once I hear country music blasting through the speakers. No shade to country music fans, it's just not what I was expecting, considering the last time I was here, they were blasting Papa Roach.

I breeze through the foyer where there are posters hanging on the walls, each promoting a different event taking place this month. Well shit, it appears Tuesday is line-dancing night. Just my fucking luck. Making my way to the bar area, I choose a spot with the best view of the club's dance floor.

"What can I get you?" the bartender asks, plopping a coaster in front of me.

I quickly scan what's on tap. "Guinness and a menu, please?"

"Sure thing." He reaches under the bar and hands me one.

As I peruse the impressive list of dishes, I hear someone cackle-laugh and look up.

You've got to be kidding me.

Mak is on the far side of the bar, her head tipped back, and she's laughing at something a blonde just said. The two of them are holding onto each other like if they let go, they'll fall off their barstools.

I grab my pint and bring it to my mouth, chugging half of it in three gulps. I've never met this woman before today and in less than twenty-four hours, this is our third encounter. It's like the universe is trying to tell me something.

Not that I believe in that Mercury swimming the Gatorade or Saturn spinning a little too far to the right stuff, but damn, it's hard to deny that something's up when this is the third encounter I've had with Mak in a twenty-four-hour period.

The bartender steps in front of my perfect view. "Decide what you want yet?"

Yeah. Mak, on her back, her legs hooked around my shoulders so I can devour her pussy thoroughly for an appetizer. "Two dozen chipotle dry rub wings, bone in, please. And the loaded nachos."

"You got it."

"Thanks." I hand over the menu, and once the bartender gets out of my way, I go back to staring at Mak. It's at this point she looks over at me from across the bar and her eyes round with surprise. Her posture stiffens, and like a tool, I lift my glass like I'm saluting her before I take another big gulp.

Her blonde friend's mouth drops, and I think it's because Mak's muttered something to her. One thing I know from a lifetime of rejection and awkwardness is to dive all in and fuck the consequences. I slide off my stool and prowl through the growing crowd of people ordering beers and mingling at the high tops.

Mak rolls her shoulders back when she sees me heading her way. An easy-going smile spreads across my face. One does on hers as well.

"Hey, Mak." I won't call her Pricurious in front of her friend. For all I know, this woman has no idea Mak's on a kink site and I'm not about to out her or give her friend a reason to pry into the name. People can be judgmental little shits, even if they're your friend.

"Hi." She clears her throat. "Leah, meet Carson the photographer. Carson, this is my best friend, Leah."

"Ohhhh the *photographer*," Leah says in a teasing way, leaning across Mak to shake my hand. "Nice to meet you. I've heard a lot about you."

Mak's cheeks blaze crimson. "Do you come here a lot?" She squeezes her eyes shut and shakes her head. "Wow, that sounded dumb. I mean, do you like the food here? This is our first time. I saw it had great reviews online and that it was new. There's never anything new in this town, you know? So boring. And since I had my hair and makeup done, I didn't want to waste it by sitting at home all night, so we decided to come here and grab some drinks. Didn't know it was line-dancing night, though. Do you line-dance?"

"Slow down, Mak truck." Leah says, sliding a drink towards her.

Mak blows out a long breath, snatches her drink, and takes several gulps. It's water with a lemon. Slamming it back on the bar, she peers up at me again. "You look nice."

She's adorable. All flustered and rambling, and out of her element. "Thanks," I say, and flick my hair to the side. "I didn't want to waste my hair and makeup either tonight."

The bad joke earns me a laugh from both of them.

"Oh, he's good. I like this one." Leah points at the open seat next to Mak. "Want to sit with us?"

"Actually…" I glance at the bartender, who's putting my food down by where I was originally sitting. "I'm going to let you two lovely ladies enjoy your night. I don't want to intrude, I just wanted to say hi."

"Oh." Leah sounds disappointed.

Mak, however, looks relieved. That cuts my pride a little, but it's okay. I took her off guard for the second time today. I couldn't just ignore her and pretend I didn't notice her here. In fact, ever since my gaze landed on her, it's like she's the only person I can see. Everyone else, including Leah, is noise and blurs. But Mak? She's a showstopper.

She's changed her outfit since this

afternoon and looks mouth-watering in her olive-green t-shirt, black jeans, and combat boots. If I don't back off now, I might even ask her to dance. "Have fun, ladies."

I make my way back to where I belong and dig into my wings and nachos. I have every intention of leaving them alone so they can enjoy their girl's night out together, but halfway through my meal, something happens that I don't like.

And all my plans change.

Chapter 8

Mak

Holy crap. I can't believe Carson is here. When I first saw him sitting across from us, my initial thought was that he followed me here. But then my more logical side figured this was the only hopping place in town tonight, and for all I know, he comes here every week for wing night. I wasn't the special chosen target. I'm just in the right place at the right time to see him again. Shit, maybe he thinks *I* stalked *him.*

It makes me question my stalker fantasies now.

And ugh. Why did I have to ramble like that? Damnit, I hate when I get nervous and start spouting off every single thought that flies through my head. It's stupid, annoying, and awkward. Carson didn't seem bothered by it, which is kind of a relief. He just threw me off guard and I panicked when he came over to us and I couldn't shut the fuck up.

Is it terrible that I almost stopped him from walking away, too? If Leah wasn't with me, I totally would have begged him to sit with me.

But Leah was making things worse instead of better because she knows all… and has had three drinks already, which means she'll *tell* all too. My blood pressure skyrocketed when she said, "Ohhh the *photographer*." Thank God she didn't follow that up with, "Mak says you're super-hot and have a really great ass and she cannot wait to fuck you."

Because that's exactly what I said to her. Among many, many other things.

But he walked away before she had a chance to spill those beans. I keep sneaking glances at him. It's like I can't look away long enough to focus on anything else. So far, I haven't caught him looking back, but I think he's keeping an eye on us. I don't know, it's just a feeling. Probably another fantasy my mind's already conjuring up to replace the stalker one.

Christ, I need a drink that's stronger than water.

"He has really big hands." Leah takes a sip of her martini. "Bet they'd make a really nice necklace."

Tell me about it. Sighing, I shake my head and look away from him. "I'm in so much trouble, aren't I?"

"Mmm depends." Leah dips her fry in ketchup. "If he's proportionate, you better get the ice pack ready, because his cock will destroy your pussy. But if he's stumpy…" Leah shrugs with a frown and chews on another fry. "I mean… he can probably still fuck you up in a nice way. Look how he eats."

I *am* looking. Carson is devouring his wings with precision. Is that even a thing? He's literally twisting the bones, pulling them out, then dunking the entire thing into sauce before popping the whole thing in his mouth in one bite. He chews nicely too. Swallows sexy.

Ooookkkkaaayyyy, I need to stop. Holy shit, this is getting worrisome. I'm legit getting hot and bothered watching a man eat a basket of hot wings. This is a new level of sexually deprived I never saw coming.

"Shit, shit, shit." Leah smacks my thigh. "Two o'clock."

I swing my gaze in the direction she's referring to. *Oh shit.* My stomach drops immediately. "Fuck my life."

"Hey," my ex says, as he leans his elbow against the bar top.

"Hey." I'd take another sip of my drink and turn my back to him as much as I can.

"What do you want?" Leah growls at him.

"Nice to see you too, Leah." He-who-can't-even-tie-his-tie-right says. "I just wanted to come say hi. See how you're doing."

"We're fine. You can leave. Mmmkay. Byeeee." Leah flicks her wrist, shooing him away.

He-who-is-a-douche-canoe ignores her. "Mak?"

I shouldn't make eye contact, but I do. "What?"

"How are you?"

"I'm doing great. How about you?" I don't care how he's doing. I just don't know how to get out of this conversation without looking like a complete bitch. For that matter, I don't know why I still care what he thinks of me.

Being a people pleaser makes me do dumb shit sometimes.

"I'm doing well." He flashes me a big smile. "I got a promotion."

"Good for you." I clear my throat, hating that I'm starting to sweat. "That's wonderful. Congratulations." *Now go away.*

"Yeah." He rubs the back of his neck and looks around. "Me and some of the boys are here celebrating. Want to join us?"

I glance over at a high-top table that has some of his colleagues surrounding it. They're all laughing and slapping each other on the back.

"No. I don't."

"Aw come on." He leans in closer. "For me?"

Anger flares in my chest, and I want to cry. I feel my face getting hot and I'm sure I look like a tomato.

Leah must sense the tension rolling off me because she jumps to my rescue. "She said no, dickhead."

"Come on. Don't be like that. It's a good night for me and I just want to celebrate."

"No one's stopping you." I manage to say. Fuck, my heart's beating so fast. "Go celebrate."

"I want to celebrate with *you*, Mak. Seeing you here makes my night even more special. Come on. You won't have to pay for a single thing. It's all on the company's dime."

"What part of the word *no* confuses you?" Leah hops off her chair.

"Relax, Leah." He touches my arm. "Mak can speak for herself."

"Which I did already," I say, even though my voice is shaking. I knock his hand off me. "I said no."

"Come on, Makayla. Don't be like that."

A warm hand rests on my shoulder, and it's not my ex's this time. "Mak." Carson's voice is rough and deep. "You ready to give me that dance now?"

My heart pounds in my throat as I gawk at Carson. He must have come up from the other side of the bar, like a sneak attack. "I..." Glancing at Leah, then He-who-gets-on-my-nerves, I lick my dry lips and nod. "Yeah. I'm ready."

I can't hop off my stool fast enough. Carson grabs my hand and gives it a squeeze before looking back at Leah. "You coming too, or am I going to have to handle this hot number all by myself?"

"Hells yes, I'm coming!" She quickly catches up with us and Carson puts his arm around her. "You're a lifesaver."

I wish she hadn't said that, even if it's kind of true. I could have gotten away from Mr. Look-at-me-I'm-so-cool on my own. However, my great escape wouldn't have been as satisfying as this one is.

His hand in mine makes me feel powerful. I squeeze it and he squeezes mine back. This man comforts me. Stupid, right? I don't know him at all, but his vibe is amazing and what he just did for us makes me crush on him harder.

We head out to the dance floor, and I notice Carson's casually glancing over towards where He-who-is-cliche is standing with his buddies. A low, rumbling growl slips out of his mouth and when he looks down at me, I find myself gravitating closer to him.

Carson is the hottest man I've ever been around in my life.

"You line dance?" Leah asks him, immediately stepping into line and going with the music.

"I don't have a clue how to line dance," Carson admits. "But I'm a quick learner and very teachable."

I smile at that. Stepping up, I count and direct him where to go, but the song ends too soon. The DJ goes straight into the Wobble by V.I.C., which makes a bunch of ladies scream and cheer, including Leah.

"YASSSS!" She throws her head back and immediately starts popping her hips to the beat.

Carson's sandwiched between us and looks lost. He keeps tripping over his own feet and can't find the beat at all. I grab his hips and yell over the music to tell him what to do. He's stiff and keeps fucking it all up but hasn't stopped trying. When it's time for us to switch direction, I place his hands on my waist and bump my ass against him. Yelling out the steps again, we're both laughing when we bop into each other because he accidentally turned the wrong way.

I don't know why I love this so much, but seeing Carson try his best to keep up makes my heart melt and pussy throb. There's something insanely hot about this man's easy-going nature. Halfway through the song, he finally gets it and my god, this man can move.

Leah howls, clapping for him. "That's what I'm talking about!"

Carson winks at me before we switch direction again. Now we're dancing side-by-side. Damn he's sexy when he thrusts his hips like he's fucking the air. This man is built for sin. I want him to move like that on top of me. And behind me. And under me.

"You weren't lying when you said you were a fast learner."

He cocks his brow and smiles while nailing the steps with the beat. I'm so hot and bothered I trip over myself, and he grabs my arm to steady me. "You good?"

I can only nod because I'm awestruck by him. Carson dominates when he wants, submits when he wants, and has the confidence of a motherfucking warlord. There's no other way to describe him.

Something in me springs to life. I grab his shirt and yank him into me. He's too tall for me to reach what I want without him bending down, so I hold him hostage, his shirt bunched in my fists and say, "Kiss me."

His brow lifts again before he lowers his mouth to mine. The instant our lips touch, I swear I go up in flames. Then Carson grabs me by my ass and lifts me off the floor. Wrapping my legs around his waist, we deepen our kiss and I feel him carrying me away. I run my fingers through his hair. He growls into my mouth. Before I know it, he's carrying me out of the damn bar like this.

"Where are we going?"

"My place." Carson's gaze sets me on fire as he puts me down. "Is that okay with you?"

"Yeah." It's more than okay. I wish we weren't wasting time outside this stupid club talking about it. "Let me just text Leah so she knows." I pull out my cell and see there's a text from her already.

LEAH: Have funnnn!

I send her a bunch of fire emojis and a

kissy face. I'd feel bad about ditching her, but I know she hates this club and only went because of me. She'd told me she had a hook up later that night anyway, so we were just killing time until her booty call showed up.

Carson pulls his keys out of his pocket. "Want to follow me there?"

"Yeah."

Turns out, we were parked next to each other in the lot.

"Holy shit, Mak." I say to myself once I'm alone in my car. "What have you gotten yourself into with this guy?"

Guess there's only one way to find out.

And my pussy can't wait.

Chapter 9

I overstepped tonight and let my emotions rule me. All my normal barriers turned to rubble when I saw that guy come up to Mak at the bar. Jealousy boiled in my gut, turning my dinner into an acid coated rock in my belly. I read his body language and hers. I heard Leah say no to him more than once. Rage threatened to consume me as I'd made my way around that fucking bar and asked Mak to dance with me.

I don't line dance.

I also don't make a scene. But the way that guy looked at what's mine made me want to shove that bottled IPA he was carrying down his goddamn throat. Instead of committing murder, I took her out of his reach.

Now she's all mine.

Glancing every couple of seconds in my rearview to make sure she's keeping up with me, I finally pull into my long driveway. It feels like a victory stretch when I turn my ignition off and hop out of my car. Mak pulls in right behind me, and I open her door just as she turns off the engine. Giving her my hand, I help her out of the car and escort her through my front door.

"Wow," she says, looking around.

"You want something to drink or anything?"

She's already making her way over to a bookshelf stocked with a variety of spicy reads and a few outliers like the autobiography she's plucked off the shelf. "You read all this?" She pulls another one out—this one's got a half-naked couple on it with a full moon in the background.

"Nah. I just collect them for the covers." I lean against the wall and cross my arms over my chest. "I took the photos for each one."

Mak gawks at me. "Really?"

"Really." I slowly prowl over to her. "I won't lie to you, Mak. Not even to impress you. And what you see is what you get with me."

I hate that I let that fly out of my face, but whatever. It's true. I'm not a muscular, zero-body-fat, six-foot-four hunk of manly man like that guy at the bar. I'm also not good at hiding my emotions. Or my insecurities, as it seems, around her.

She bends down and pulls out a comic book. "Did you do this too?"

"Nah. That was just art I had to have."

"Hmmm." She flicks through the pages. "Zombie Tramp." She looks back on the shelf. "You only have three?"

"I'm not really into comics." I shrug. "But these ones looked cool, so I got them."

Mak runs her fingers over the comic character's tits. "I think if I had a rack like this, I'd wear this same outfit."

"You'd look hotter than her in that outfit, for sure."

"Awww, Carson, are you saying I'm hotter than a decaying corpse with winged eyeliner?" We both start laughing and she slides the comic back in its place on the shelf. "Your house is really cool. It's so different from your studio."

"That was the point." I make my way across the living room, loving that she's following me. "My head never turns off and I crave different things, including atmospheres. Work is all urban, clean lines and neon lights. Home is eclectic, old, and stuffy."

"It's not stuffy. It's comfy."

I light the fireplace and rub my palms together. "Glad you think so."

She plops down on the sofa and curls up like she lives here. "Thanks for earlier."

I make sure to keep my expression impassive as I sit next to her. "You're welcome." I want to ask if I've overstepped. I want to explain myself. I want to find out what that guy was saying to upset her. But I don't pry. And it no longer matters. She's here with me and this is where she'll stay for as long as she wants.

"That was my ex."

So much for it not mattering. "Oh yeah?" My throat's closing up. Jealousy coils in my belly again and it makes no sense. Why am I feeling like an animal who wants to mark his territory?

"He's a total douchebag."

I sense there's more she wants to say and is afraid to. I don't want her to keep things from me only because she's afraid of my reaction. She doesn't owe me an explanation or her backstory. We're nowhere near that level of intimacy yet. But if her anxieties impact our dynamic, then I want to know about them so we can work through it.

"I take it he's not good with the word no." It's all I can bring myself to say. I'm honestly scared of what she'll tell me next. My mind's racing with situations and none of them are okay.

Mak brings her knees up to her chest and wraps her arms around them. "He's very… persuasive."

"You mean he's *coercive*."

"Yes."

My hands ball into fists and I'm sure the veins in my temples are protruding. I need to calm down. The fact that she's being this open so soon is amazing. I can't ruin it.

Dipping my face closer hers to get full eye contact, I hold Mak's gaze. "I respect the word no more than any other word." I give her a moment to let that sink in. "As part of our dynamic, you'll see that my actions—and inactions—will speak for themselves. But we will also have a safe word in place." Like normal, I've gone into professional mode because I have no clue how else to respond. "Coercion is not consent. That goes for both parties."

She nods and looks down at the floor. It's not submission, it's a mix of shame, fear, and uncertainty I sense in her body language. That bugs me. A lot.

Getting up off the couch, I squat down in front of her. "I have to be honest with you, Makayla. And you have to be honest with me. You can change your mind at any time and walk away from this." I really hope she doesn't. "And at any point, you can call your safe word and the game is over."

She pales and her hazel eyes turn a little glassy. "Game?"

"The scene," I correct. "You read my profile before you signed the contract, right?"

"Yes."

"All of it?"

"Yes."

"And all of the contract?"

"Yes."

Good. "Then you know I get off on making my sub come. I also get off on chasing you and pinning you down. Marking you with bites and scratches. I like being extremely physical and the more you play with me and the more you fight back or faster you run, the harder I'll want to fuck you."

I really need a lesson on how to talk to women because this is likely not it. She's just come down from a vulnerable moment and I went straight into talking about chasing, pinning, and fucking her. Someone should castrate me.

"Cupcake," she says. I must look confused because she follows that up with, "My safe word is Cupcake."

My smile nearly splits my face. "Cupcake it is."

She blows out a shaky breath, but at least she's smiling again. "What's yours?"

Bless her soul. "I'll use Cupcake too, just to keep it simple." Never in my life have I had to use a safe word for myself.

"Okay." Her brow furrows. "And the minute one of us says it, everything stops?"

"Immediately." I notice she's hanging on my answer like a fucking prayer, and that doesn't sit well with me. I have a feeling Mr. Coercive did things he shouldn't have with my girl. "Use the word the instant you start feeling uncomfortable or anxious about what we're doing. Or if you're in pain or are scared." I wait for her to nod again. "We'll stop and go over what the problem is and if there's a way to fix it, fine. If not, we stop the scene and that's the end."

Her face is red, and eyes are round like I've said something she doesn't want to hear.

"The end of the scene, Mak, not of our partnership. Unless, of course, you want that too. But there won't be any hard feelings on my end if you use the safe word. Ever. It's important and should be used. Everyone has a limit and if you don't know what that limit is, then it's even more important to say 'cupcake' if something's bothering you."

She chews on her bottom lip. Once again, I feel like I'm saying things in the wrong order, but I can't help myself. This is how I'm made. Some guys are all suave and confidence—*looking at you, Trey*—and others have the dominant gene times ten that they can balance with humor—*cough, cough* Glitch *cough, cough*—but I don't have those things.

I have brutal honesty.

Mak stares into the crackling fire for a moment. I give her some space and back off, busying myself by adding more wood to the small hearth. This old house has a lot of charm, but it's also hard to keep comfortable in. Too cold in winter, too hot in summer. Still, my hardwood floors are original to the house and so are the beams above us in the living room. I love my home, but right now I want fresh air.

And I want to strip Mak out of her clothes and fuck her against every surface I can reach.

I'm an animal sometimes. With Mak in my space, I'm going to be an animal more often than not.

I hope she can handle me. Turning my back to her, I figure I should lay out more ground rules. "How long have you been into primal play, Mak?"

"A little while now." She's crept up behind me without my realizing it. Her hands are icy when she runs her fingers along the cords of muscle in my arms. "I felt your eyes on me at the club. I kept trying to catch you looking at me and couldn't, but I know you were watching me."

I'm still as stone.

"I also didn't see or hear you creep up behind us when you asked me to dance."

I swallow hard.

"But I was never more relieved to have you behind me like that."

I can't feel my feet.

"You're a big guy." She runs her hands up my chest and my insecurities try to claw my confidence to shreds. "That's a massive turn on, Carson."

I turn to face her. "I'm nothing like your ex."

Fuck, why did I have to say that?

"I'm glad, because he was a pussy." Mak scrapes her nails across my pecs. "I'm hoping you're a beast."

Hoping? "I'm a fucking animal when I want to be, Mak." And part of me is worried she won't be able to handle that.

"Do you want to be an animal right now, Carson?" She tips her head like a cat studying a mouse.

How the fuck did I just become the mouse? "Do *you* want me to be an animal?"

"I wouldn't have signed that contract otherwise."

True. But that was before she saw me in person. Before she kissed me. Before she touched me.

Speaking of which, I can't believe I haven't felt nauseous with her hands on me like this. Usually, I have to fight to let a woman touch me without my asking, but Mak's fingers have zero boundaries and I find myself craving for her to keep going.

I step closer to her and tower over her. She's a petite thing. Maybe five-foot-two in those boots. I'm six-three and the height difference feels a lot bigger considering I'm easily a hundred and fifty pounds heavier than her. And that's being conservative.

"I like a man who can throw his weight around," she says to me. "I want someone who can tackle me down and pin me... who can crush me if he wanted to, but won't."

That's me. I'm that guy.

"I want someone who can douse me with

fear and lust at the same time. Who keeps me safe and spikes my adrenaline in the same breath." She runs her hand up to my throat and wraps her dainty little fingers around my neck. "I want someone who shows me how to live wildly." She tips her head to the side again. "Are you that someone, Carson?"

My dick is so fucking hard I can't move.

"Answer me. Because if it's yes, then we're going to have a lot of fun together. If it's a no, I'll leave now. No harm, no foul."

I quickly knock her hand off my throat and step forward. She steps back, her mouth parted a little as if she might squeak. I prowl after her as she keeps moving backwards until her ass hits my front door.

A growl slips from my lips. "You sure about this, Mak?"

"Yes." Her pupils are huge. There are still things we need to lay out, but I'll be damned if I'm going to let this moment slip through my fingers because I want to play by the rules and do things like I've always done them.

"Last chance," I warn, pressing my palms against the door, caging her in.

"I want this, Carson. I want *you*."

"Bare or covered?" I'm shocked I have the brain cells to make this conversation. All my blood has gone to my rock-hard dick.

"What?"

I grab my cock and shove my groin

forward. "Am I fucking you raw or not, Mak?"

"Umm. Yes?"

"Is that a question or an answer?"

"Both."

I step back. Normally I'd nip her neck and grope all the pretty pieces of her body I want to come all over, but she's been coerced before into things she didn't want to do, and I'll be damned if I'll put her in a position where she can't think straight enough to answer honestly.

"Come with me." Grabbing her hand, all the tension binding tightly around us snaps free. I bring her into the kitchen and pour us both a glass of water. "Sit."

She plops down on the chair and looks a little angry and confused.

I hand her over a glass of water. "Drink."

Mak snatches it from my hand and gulps it down. Then she slams the empty glass on the table and leans back in her chair with her arms crossed. Brows furrowed, and mouth turned down, she grumbles, "Want me to bark like a dog next?"

That makes me smile. Her sarcasm will cost her later. "I need you to think clearly. What just happened was my fault. I got ahead of myself. We need parameters first."

If she was going to disagree with who was to blame, she stops herself and that makes me happy. Two things are iron clad in this dynamic: One, I'm the dominant. Two, she holds all the power.

I need to make sure that we're on the same page before I set us both loose on each other.

"As per the K!nkLink requirements, both of us have been tested and are clean." I sip my water. "I'm perfectly comfortable letting you decide if I can fuck you raw or with a condom. And again, this preference can change at any time."

She only stares at me.

"I need your answer before we continue."

"I…" She fiddles with her fingers.

I know I'm making her nervous, but for once that's okay. This is important, and she needs to take everything I say seriously. "You don't have to answer me right now, but nothing will happen between us until boundaries are set. I apologize for my behavior in the living room. It's just…" Here comes my brutal honesty and transparency again. "I've been thinking about fucking you for the past twenty-four hours and now that I have you in my house, I want nothing more than to strip you down and worship every inch of your body. I shouldn't have taken things as far as I did in the living room before we set up clear boundaries and for that, I'm sorry."

Her brows pinch together, and mouth falls open.

"Until we are on the same page, I won't touch you again."

Silence grows between us. My ears start

ringing. My dick hurts because it's losing blood flow in my jeans, but I use that pain to focus. It's the least I can do since I nearly went overboard in the living room just now.

See? This is why it's important to have rules. I can't believe I broke so many of mine tonight.

Her voice cracks a little when she says, "Bare."

"Where can I come?"

She glances at her empty glass for a moment, then those gorgeous hazels lift up to meet my gaze. "Anywhere you want."

"What about anal?"

"I…" She bites her plump bottom lip. "I only tried it once, and it hurt. I didn't like it."

That's not a yes or a no. I need one or the other. "Are you willing to try it again?"

"Yes," she says without hesitation. "So long as I can use my safe word if I don't like it."

She doesn't get it. Mak still can't grasp the purpose of a safe word if she felt the need to say that to me. "I want you to use it, Mak. At any point. At any time. I don't care if I'm mid orgasming inside your cunt, you say Cupcake and I will pull out and stop instantly."

Her cheeks turn pink again. "Okay."

"Okay, what?"

"I want anal. When I'm ready, I'll ask you for it."

She's not going to ask. She's going to beg.

"I want you to come all over me," she continues. "I like rough, messy sex. Cum play. Breath play. I want you to bite me and bruise me and sometimes choke me out when you make me come."

My entire body locks up hearing her demands. "I can do all that." Happily. "But I won't hit you violently. That's a hard limit for me." If she needs extreme pain to get off, we might not be the match I think we are. Spanking, however, is always on my list of things I'll do.

"I don't want you to hit me. But, you said you'd pin me down. Bite me. I want marks on my body from you, so the next day I can think about what we did."

Sweet mother of glory, I can smell her arousal from here. Fuuuuuck. I breathe through my mouth so I can keep my focus. The scent of a woman's cunt is a massive turn on for me. I wish I could bathe in that scent. Pussy is divine.

"Okay." Shit, my voice is deep and gruff.

"What about you?" She leans back in her chair. "What do you want?"

My gaze deadlocks hers. "Everything you're willing to give me, Mak." I lean in and growl like a starved animal. Her pupils dilate and I enjoy watching her pulse throb in her neck. "And I want you to run."

"N-now?"

I growl again as my answer.

Her cheeks pinken and eyes grow wide as

a smile spreads across her sweet face. Suddenly, Mak stands so fast she knocks her chair over. Then my beautiful vixen books it out of the kitchen, through my living room, and out the front door.

Game. On.

Chapter 10

Mak

This is crazy!

I can't believe I'm doing this. I can't believe I'm excited that I'm doing this. As I beat feet across the front lawn, I have no clue where the hell I'm supposed to go. There are no neighbors that I can see. Carson lives next to a farm, but that's so far off, I can barely make out the structure. All I can see are pastures and fences. There's a huge shed out back to my left, and woods curve around the other side of his property. I have no clue how much of this land he owns.

And right now, I don't care.

Carson stands at the door and points towards the woods.

Holy shit. We're really doing this.

I must be nuts to be so turned on. Shouldn't I be scared? Worried? It's like my self-preservation has turned off because really all I want is for him to come at me, lift me into his arms, and ravage me.

I want him to tear my clothes off and hold

me down and—

Fuck, he's coming!

I book it towards the woods, relieved I have my boots on. It's freezing out, and white puffs form from my heavy breaths. I can't see out here, it's too dark, but something snaps inside my brain, and I get quiet. Pressing my back against a big tree, I squint and look around to figure out where to go next.

Adrenaline pumps in my veins so fast, I feel a little dizzy.

This is scary and fun, and I have no clue how to handle it. It's nothing like I read about. It's a million times more intense. There's a level of danger to this I didn't realize. Maybe that element is here because I don't really know Carson. Maybe it's because this is my first time being chased by an actual primal Dom.

Maybe it's because this is a mistake, and I should run for my car and hightail it out of here because what if Carson's a murderer who poses as a Dom and takes pictures of his victims at his boudoir studio for souvenirs before he kills them and shoves them in his basement like a real Zombie Tramp collection?

Get a grip, Mak. I squeeze my eyes shut and breathe. I have a safe word. I'll use it if I have to.

Call me reckless, but I trust Carson. He seems so open and transparent. And he's taking this "situationship" very seriously. I can tell it's not just a fantasy for him, but a true lifestyle.

I'm the one learning as I go here.

Footsteps crunch against the fallen leaves as he makes his way towards where I'm hiding. Instead of sitting still, I dash between the trees. This is exhilarating. Before I make it to another hiding spot, I realize I want him to catch me. I want to make it easy for him, but not too easy.

Unfortunately, I'm so wrapped in my head that I don't hear him coming until it's too late.

"Shit!" I trip over a fallen branch, my arms pinwheeling as I keep running in the direction of a clearing. I think I must have made a huge circle in the woods because I see the back of Carson's house and deck light.

I sense him before I feel him.

He grabs my waist and lifts me up. I thought he'd tackle me, which is what I've braced for, but as my legs go up in the air and the sky spins, I see I made the wrong assumption. Carson swings me around and slams me against a tree—not too hard, but not gently either—and we're both panting.

"What's your safe word, Mak?"

His voice is gruff and deep. Shifter fantasies start firing off in my imagination and my pussy clenches. "Cupcake."

"Good girl." He nudges his knee between my legs and pins my arms above my head. "This stops whenever you want it to. Just say your word."

I clamp my mouth shut because there's no

fucking way I'm saying it. I don't want this to stop. I've never been so turned on in my life and we've barely done a damned thing yet.

Carson kisses my throat column, alternating between licks and nips. Heat floods my pussy. I want to run my fingers through his thick black hair. I want to press his head down to my cunt. But when I try to twist out of his hold, his grip tightens on my wrists.

My adrenaline spikes again.

Carson's strong. I'm at his mercy.

So why do I feel like I'm the one with all the power?

Testing our limits, I raise my knee up and half-heartedly kick him. He backs off just enough to loosen his grip and give me breathing space. "Again," he orders.

I kick him a little harder this time and he backs away a few more steps. There's a fraction of a second where I hesitate and then I take off again—this time across the lawn.

Carson's right behind me in a matter of heartbeats and he does tackle me this time, only he softens the fall by twisting around, so I land on top of him. His arms are big and muscular, caging me in as we roll across the frosty grass. I land on the bottom, out of breath and smiling as Carson keeps himself from crushing me.

His weight presses against my body in a delicious way. I could wiggle out from under him if I wanted. He's giving me every opportunity to get away from him, but I would never.

Fuck that.

I wrap my arms around his neck and lift up to crush my mouth against his. Blood pumps loudly in my ears. I'm shaking and can't tell if it's the thrill of this moment, or the icy cold temps of the night.

I feel dizzy again.

Carson runs his hand through my hair, holding himself up with his other arm, and presses his groin to mine. He's so hard. I want to feel him inside me. Breaking our kiss first, he bites my neck a little harder than before.

"Fuck me," I beg.

Carson growls against my ear before he bites down on my earlobe. The sting of his teeth makes electricity zip down my limbs. "Not this time," he says in a low, gravelly voice.

The rejection makes my stomach drop.

"Do you know why the big bad wolf is the real hero, Mak?" He unbuttons my fly and pulls my jeans down. "It's because he can hear you better…" He lowers down and kisses my belly. "See you better…" He grabs my panties with his teeth and pulls them down over my thighs. "And *eats* you better."

I'm laying back on the frosted ground with my boot heels digging into this man's back and my fucking pants are down around my ankles. I feel like I've trapped Carson between my legs and—

"Holy *fuck*." My hands immediately grip his head to keep him right where he is.

Carson's tongue should have a warning label. Scratch that, this entire man should come with a warning label: *Will break you and make you beg him to do it again.*

My eyes cross as he sucks on my clit and shoves a finger inside me. I feel swollen and soaked and super sensitive and lightheaded. He fucks me with his finger and sucks my clit with just enough pressure to make me spiral into a fast-approaching orgasm that tears through me so hard I see stars.

"That's my good girl," he says from between my thighs.

My jaw drops when he rubs his face all over my slick pussy. I'm talking this man literally smears my cum all over his mouth, chin, and cheeks. Then he slides the tip of his nose up and down the seam of my cunt before flicking my clit with his tongue again.

"Holy shit," I groan. This is wild. I try to wiggle away so I can have a second to recuperate, but Carson grabs my hips and holds me in place.

"Give me more of your cum." He jerks me forward and tilts my bottom half until my legs are a tangled mess in the air, my knees spread, and ass and pussy on display.

It's vulgar and vulnerable and I'm so here

for it.

Carson cups my ass cheeks and tips me up so he can lick my pussy again. While he wreaks havoc on my body, I try to figure out how the hell I got to this place.

God bless K!nkLink. I'm buying stock in that app.

He starts fingering me again, and this time it feels deeper. More aggressive. Holding my breath, I pay attention to every sensation running through my body — the tightness coiling in my belly, how the muscles in my calves flex, the way the hard, cold ground bites my back, the chill on my cheeks, the second finger he's shoving into me, the way my heart pounds, the feeling of his teeth grazing my clit. The sensations stack up. Pressure builds.

"Oh shit, oh fuck, oh my —"

I come again, a million times harder this round. Heels against his back, I arch back and thrust upwards until my ass lifts out of his hands. I feel like I'm floating. Carson seals his mouth over my clit again and drags his hot tongue all over my pussy, as if gathering every drop of pleasure he's just wrung out of me.

I've never felt so free in my life.

"That's it." Carson licks me again. "Give me all you fucking got."

Pumping his fingers inside me harder and faster, I'm no longer able to see straight. Dots dance in my vision and I feel a little nauseous.

It's confusing and exhilarating, but I don't like it. "Cupcake."

Carson pulls away instantly and cushions my ass with his hands while I sink my bottom half back onto the ground. Then he untangles himself from my legs and sits back on his haunches to give me space. "Good girl," he says with a smile.

I don't feel good. I feel like I just ruined this whole thing. And now I don't like being out here and I'm confused and need to leave. Tugging up my pants, my throat tightens, and it hurts to swallow.

"Talk to me, Mak."

Carson's not coming close to me, and I hate that too.

"I…" Tears spring from my eyes and I can't understand my actions at all.

"I've got you," he says, scooping me up. "You did so good, Mak. I'm so fucking proud of you."

"But that doesn't make sense," I say as he carries me onto his deck and back into the house. The sliding glass door slams shut behind us and I feel guilty and don't know why. "I just ruined the whole scene."

"You didn't ruin a damned thing, sweet vixen. You did exactly what you should have done." He sets me on his couch and drops down in front of me. Rubbing his big palms over my thighs, his smile is warm and genuine. "You trusted me enough to play with you. You also used your safe word when you felt you should. Thank you."

Why is he thanking me?

I swipe my tears away, feeling stupid for acting like this. "I feel like I should be the one to thank you. I've..." Emotions swarm me and none of them make sense. "I've never come like that in my life. I never felt so much at once before."

Carson nods, like he gets what I'm saying. "Sometimes emotions can sneak up on you. Especially if you're in a different head space."

"Why am I crying like this? I feel confused and weird." And foolish because holy crap, he's never going to want to play with me again if I act like this. I'm a basket case.

"I think you're dropping." He rubs the back of his neck. "I'm going to get you some water and snacks, okay? I'll be right back."

I nod because what else am I supposed to do?

He shoots off to the kitchen and comes back less than a minute later with a bottle of water, a bag of chips, and some cookies. "Here," he hands them over. "Let me just get you comfy first." I take the snacks, and then he's suddenly putting a blanket around my shoulders and another across my lap. "Better?"

His tone is soft and gentle, and I can't believe this is happening. I've never dropped before. I don't think I understand what a drop even is. It's nothing like what I've experienced with other lovers.

"Yes. Thank you." My stomach twists when he walks away to poke at the fire that's died down. "Can you sit with me?"

"Absolutely." Carson throws another log on the flames, then wipes his hands on his jeans before easing down on the couch next to me. "Want to watch TV?"

"No." Maybe I should have said yes, but my answer flew out automatically and I really don't want to watch anything. Dread settles in my belly. "Can you explain to me why I'm acting like this?"

"Your body has released a ton of endorphins and adrenaline. The endorphins make you feel euphoric while the adrenaline keeps your body going through the scene. When those things leave your system quickly, you drop. Sometimes the chemicals make you go from happy to sad and lonely. It's different for everyone."

"Do you ever feel like this?"

"I've experienced Dom drop a few times. I didn't see it coming, to be honest, and my partner and I were not prepared for it." He runs his hands through his hair as if he's a little agitated. "It was a rookie mistake back then. And I can't believe I made it again now."

He thinks I'm a mistake? Great.

"I'm so sorry, Mak." He shakes his head and his big brown eyes lock onto mine. "I should have done better tonight. I'm not sure where I fucked up."

"It's not you, it's me."

"No, Mak. As your Dom, I should have—"

My confession flies out of my mouth so fast, it's all one word. "I've-never-done-any-of-this-before."

The air whooshes out of him. His chest falls and shoulders drop as a mixture of disappointment and anger twists his face into a scowl. "You *lied* on your profile?"

"My name is Pricurious. We went over that. I'm *curious* about it."

He turns to face me fully. "But your profile listed that your biggest kink was primal. When we spoke in the chat, I even asked you to verify it. You said you were into primal and that you were curious." He scrubs his face and utters a long stream of cuss words into his palms. "Fuck, Mak."

Instead of scolding me or yelling at me or kicking me out like I expect him to, Carson scoops me into his lap and holds me.

"I'm sorry," I whisper. "You probably think I was lying or tricking you, but I wasn't. I'm into primal. I just haven't had a chance to really experience it until tonight."

His tone is clipped. "I went into this thinking you might not have had a lot of experience with this, but I didn't think you had *none*. If I'd known, I would have been much more careful with you."

"You *were* careful with me." Far more than I anticipated. "I loved it."

And I can't believe I ended it so fast. Carson never even got to come. He never even got to take his shirt off, for fuck's sake.

"If you'd have been open and honest with me, Mak, we'd have started this dynamic a different way. I would have played with you first. Bit and wrestled, kissed and nipped."

"You did all that."

"Yeah, *after* tearing through the woods after you."

He's said it like that's the wrong thing to have done. I disagree. "I loved every bit of it. I'm no longer Pricurious, I've evolved to Pri-big-fan-of-WolfByte."

He doesn't laugh at my bad joke. I feel awful for leading him to believe I could keep up with his level of experience this soon. "I'm sorry."

"We need to always be open and honest. Do you understand me?"

"Yes." It's my fault for not coming clean sooner. But if I had, he would have held back, and I didn't want that to happen. "If I'd been upfront and said I was completely inexperienced, it would have caused me to overthink my choices."

"Being careful is important. It's okay to question your choices, Mak."

"Not for me, it isn't. I talk myself out of everything and regret it later. I'm not willing to do that with me and you. I want full-on wild, or nothing at all."

As silence spreads between us, I curl against his chest, and we relax into each other.

Burying his face in the crook of my neck, Carson's breath tickles my collarbone when he softly says, "You gave me a very precious gift tonight, Mak." He pulls back when I look up at him and he swipes the hair from my face. "You trusted me with your first time. Thank you."

I'm starting to understand exactly how important open honesty is for this dynamic. "Thanks for making it spectacular."

He hugs me tighter. "We'll go slower next time, okay? And I'm going to need to know ways you prefer I give you the best aftercare."

"This is pretty nice." I rest my cheek on his shoulder. "The cookies are good too."

He grabs the package of cookies from where I'd just been sitting. "Here." He tears open the top and offers one to me. I take it with my teeth and put the whole cookie in my mouth at once. Carson's eyebrows raise. "That's impressive."

While chewing my cookie, I feel a little better. Maybe it's the way he's holding me. Maybe it's the sugar. Maybe I'm just finally understanding myself a little more. "Carson?"

"Yeah?"

"I don't want to go slower." I press my lips to his and pull his shirt off.

Chapter 11

Carson

This is nuts. I keep breaking all my goddamn rules and it's not going to end well between Mak and me if I don't get a handle on my self-control and do better than this. I've slipped up countless times already.

But it feels good to not be rigid for once. And when she runs her nails down my chest, I love how my body erupts with goosebumps and my nipples harden. My dick is like a steel pipe in my jeans. Even after all of this, I'm still hard and ready to fuck.

That makes me feel guilty for reasons I can't explain.

I should have done more homework on Mak before bringing her here. I should have made sure we both understood what scene would happen first before we began. But it's her fault that she wasn't open with me and as honest as she should have been about her experience level.

Now she knows.

I hope she's learned her lesson because I

don't want to teach her another one. This night has truly rocked me to my core. Part of me wants to teach her everything about primal kink so she can go out into the world and live her best life. Another part of me wants to keep her to myself and spoil her rotten before and after I chase her down and fuck her senseless.

But a bigger part of me is leery of what this might grow into.

I know we signed a contract. I know this is just a partnership. I know it's temporary.

But it doesn't feel that way.

It feels real. It feels alive and warm and pulsing and fated—which is preposterous. Love isn't in the cards for me. This is just a phase. I'm going through something; I just can't tell what it is. And I'm going to take Mak on this ride with me because I'll be damned if I'm going to set her loose and let anyone else enjoy her sweet mouth, greedy hands, or her divine pussy.

Her scent remains on my mouth, nose, chin, and cheeks. I can smell her every time I breathe.

And now she's pulling my shirt off and telling me she doesn't want to go slow.

What the fuck am I supposed to do with that?

Not this.

Not what I'm doing right now.

I sit up so she can pull my shirt all the way off. I don't have six-pack abs like the models on the covers of the books on my shelf. I don't have a small waist with that V-shaped muscle that makes women foam at the mouth. I'm strong and solid as a tank with lots of extra cushion.

She runs her hands down my torso and I grip her wrist when she gets too close to my love handles. My jaw clenches. There's a question in her eyes I'm not about to answer. Talk about being a hypocrite. I just lectured her about open honesty and here I am, hiding my own demons.

My insecurities have roared to life, and I feel trapped and at her mercy. Feeling vulnerable sucks, but it's something I'm forever actively working on. Which is why I let her wrist go and lean back so she can have a good look at me.

Being on display makes me vicious. "I'm nothing like your ex."

Mak's gaze locks with mine and I feel like her hazel eyes are swallowing me whole. "I really hope that's true," she whispers.

Instead of firing off questions to dig deeper into that comment, I let it go for now. We've been on strange, rocky ground and I'd hate to fuck this up more than I already have.

The chemistry between us feels natural. Her touch on my body does too. I don't quiver or shrink back when she runs her hands all over me again. In fact, I press into it. I want it.

I crave it.

I've never been the exposed one before. I

can't tell if I like it or not, but Mak's body language tells me everything I need to know. She's curious and turned on, and that's all because of me.

She wants *me*.

Not just the thrill of the chase or the promise of a good, hard fuck.

Me.

There's an ache in my chest—a warning that I'm in so much fucking trouble. Grappling for a little control, I skate my hands up her back and wind her long hair around my palm, tangling it in my fingers to give it a tug. Her smile is brighter than the sun. Warmth floods my system, melting my icy resolve.

Scenes come with intimacy and exposure, but they're still just scenes. A chapter in a book. A fantasy set in reality. It's a bubble that eventually pops. And I'm always the one in charge.

But this feels different. No safe word will save me from the feelings creeping up to darken my thoughts. No chase through the woods will expel this type of energy from my body.

Freaked out, I make my move. Smashing my lips to hers, I grab her ass and lift her so I can stand and free myself from her cage. Except instead of putting her down and stepping away like I plan, I groan into her mouth as she wraps her legs around me tighter.

She wants me.

Those three words sound unreal in my head.

She doesn't want you. She wants the thrill. This is new and exciting and she's using you to experiment with. Just like all the others. That's it. This is just pretend. It's only temporary.

My heart cracks.

Mak pulls away long enough to say, "You're so damn sexy, Carson."

I almost drop her. If it wasn't for the scent of her arousal still stuck in my nose from earlier, I think I would have kicked her out of my house for saying that.

Instead, my hands grow hungry for her. I no longer have to hold on to her because Mak's clinging to me like she's part of my ribcage, keeping my heart locked inside. Her tiny noises and intoxicating scent makes my blood run hot. Scraping my short fingernails down her back, I growl at her. She's so little compared to me. I've never been with someone her size before. It makes me even more aware of how big I am.

And how careful I need to be.

She's beautiful and precious, and I want to devour her. I don't care that she's probably using me to explore her limits with. I don't care that she'll eventually leave me in the dust. I don't care that I can't seem to follow my own rules. I don't care, I don't care, I don't fucking care.

I want this woman so badly I could scream.

"I want you." We both say at the same time.

It's like those three words create a frenzy between us. I start making our way to the staircase so I can bring her to my bedroom until she says, "Here. Right here on the steps."

Is she for real?

"Now, Carson."

"Yes, ma'am." No one's ever wanted me bad enough to not be willing to wait another second to have me. Christ, I think I'm blushing.

Kissing her hard, I remind myself that she's still in a drop. She could very well be trying to climb out or mask it, but no one pulls out of a drop with a hug and a cookie. We're new to each other, which means I'm in unchartered territory and better tread carefully.

Still, I don't want to stop this, even though I know damn well it's the right thing to do.

Which means I'll take my cues from her and make sure I pay attention to every noise and move she makes. If I sense she's struggling, I'll stop everything. Her body language has been, so far, crystal clear. Pulling her shirt off, I manage to spin myself around and sit on the steps with her between my legs.

"You're stunning, Mak." All feral and keyed up, so ready to fuck, I palm her tits and bite her nipples through the fabric of her bra. She's not top heavy, which I like. I'm an ass man.

"Take off your pants," she orders as I scratch down her back again.

"Take them off yourself." I bite her nipple a little harder this time, relishing how her breath catches.

Mak starts fumbling with my belt buckle and I look down to watch. The sight of my gut causes me to freeze. *Shit.* Squeezing my eyes shut, I hate that I can't let go of my past long enough to enjoy this for more than a few seconds. It's ridiculous.

She springs my button and zipper free, and I lift my hips to help her out. Mak yanks my jeans down and I toe off my boots so she can pull them all the way off if she wants to. She slips my jeans down, taking my boxers with them, and tosses both onto the floor.

"Holy Hell Hounds, Batman." Her gaze drops to my cock and then back up to my face. "Lucifer sent you, didn't he?"

"Excuse me?"

"Satan had to have sent you here to destroy my soul and my pussy. You can't convince me otherwise."

"Better say your prayers then." I press my palm on the top of her head. "On your knees works best."

She lowers down and opens her mouth to swallow half my dick down her throat. Swear to fuck, I can't move for a solid thirty seconds. This woman sucks cock like she's trying to get boba out of a skinny straw. Holy shit. Which one of us was sent by Satan again? Not me.

It's her. Definitely her.

Thank you, Lucifer. I will be forever grateful for this gift.

I've been so wound up all night that it's not going to take me very long before I blow my load down her throat. She's slurping and gagging and going all out and fffffffuck me I'm gonna come.

"Swallow me." I thrust my hips up, and she gags a little as I drive more of myself down her throat. Pressure builds at the base of my spine, a sheen of sweat bursts across my chest and forehead. Before I explode, I yank her head back and my dick falls out of her mouth with a plop. "On second thought," I say, breathless. "Get your ass up those stairs so I can fuck you properly."

She wipes the drool off her chin with the back of her hand. "But you said to swallow you."

"You will." I stand up and move out of the way so she has access to the rest of the staircase. "When I'm ready for you to."

Tipping my head, I silently give her the go signal. Mak squeaks as she slips past me, but doesn't make it very far. I almost worry she's changed her mind until I see that she's kicking her boots off and tossing them over the railing. While I watch with bated breath, she strips on the stairs, a little out of my reach.

"There." She tosses all her clothes over the railing too. "Now we're even."

I catch up to her in seconds. We're at the very top by the time I wrap my arm around her waist and hold her in place. Bumping the back of her knees with mine, she crumbles in my arms, laughing while I make her sink onto all fours.

"Ass up, little vixen." I slap her pert cheeks before spreading them.

"Carson, what are you..." She grunts and tips forward. "Holy moly."

I tongue her sweet pussy and my dick throbs for a taste. I can't hold back, nor do I want to. Growling, I hold her hips with one hand and position my cock against her entrance with the other. She's soaked and smells divine. I press the fat tip of my dick against her pussy and shove inside an inch at a time.

I wish I could take a picture of how pretty her cunt looks wrapped around my cock. I'm not even a third of the way in when my diabolical woman shoves backwards, forcing me to bottom out.

"Fuck, you're tight." My knees dig into the steps as I fuck her from behind. Our bodies slap together and there's a ringing in my ears.

She's so perfect. So beautiful. So fun and trusting. "You." *Slam!* "Belong." *Slam!* "To me." *Slam!*

"Yes." Mak groans as her body rocks back

and forth from my hard thrusts.

My pace quickens, and balls draw up tight. That beautiful pressure comes back at the base of my spine and my heart feels like it might explode. I keep one knee on the step and bring my other foot up to the landing she's on. My girl screams when I fuck her at this new angle.

I stop. "Too deep?"

"No." Mak pants, looking over her shoulder at me. Her cheeks are bright pink, and lips are swollen. "Just… give me a second to adjust." I don't make a move and wait for her guidance. When she slowly presses back against me again and rocks herself on my shaft, I'm all for letting her take the lead. Before long, she's bucking hard and fast against me. Her arousal coats my dick, and my eyes roll back when I smell it.

Women have a fragrance that could start galactic wars. It makes men like me turn into feral animals.

Holding her hips, I thrust harder and harder.

"More," she begs. "I want harder."

I press my chest against her back, forcing her to lie flat on her belly at the top of the landing. "How about I go deeper, little vixen." I slam into her from this new angle and Mak claws the floorboards.

I can't wait for her to do that to my back later.

With me on top, I feel more like myself and want to give my girl the fuck of a lifetime. That's not going to happen on a set of steps. I pull out and smack her ass, loving how it jiggles and turns red with my handprint. She's so wet, her thighs are glistening from it.

I let out a low, long growl that draws her attention to me. Her eyes are big and mouth is parted as I let the growl drag out for as long as possible. With my eyes locked on hers, I shove a finger in her pussy to gather her arousal, and then point to my bedroom. "Crawl through that door and get on my bed."

I suck my finger clean while watching Mak obey me. She doesn't crawl so much as scramble through my bedroom door. *Such a good girl.*

"Holy shit," she says the instant she's in there.

I smile to myself, knowing exactly what she's looking at.

Chapter 12

Mak

Did I die and go to BDSM heaven? Is there such a place? If so, it's gotta be Carson's bedroom.

The first thing I see is a king-sized bed with black sheets. The second thing I see is a wall of floggers. A wall. An entire wall of floggers and crops and cuffs and things I've never seen before. The display looks more like art than toys.

"See something you like?" Carson leans against the doorjamb, his arms stretched above him and his hard dick juts straight out towards me.

"Yeah." My gaze drags up and down his body. "I see *you*."

These toys might be fun to play with on some other day, but right now, I want Carson to finish what he started. I want him to fuck me and come in my mouth. Standing on shaky legs, I make my way over to him. Wow, my pussy is swollen. It feels all puffed out and I cup it on instinct.

Carson's brows dig down. "Are you sore?"

"Not at all."

He closes the space between us and gracefully drops to his knees. Gently pulling my hand away, he kisses my pussy, not seeming to care that I'm not groomed very well. It makes me suddenly very self-conscious. Were his other subs waxed and perfectly smooth, or natural, or some shape in between?

Why do I even care?

"Your scent drives me wild, Mak." Carson buries his face in my cunt and licks it. I'm too sensitive and flinch out of his tongue's reach. Without saying a word, he arches an eyebrow as he looks up at me. His lips are shiny, and I wonder what I taste like on his mouth.

Bending down, I kiss him until we're both mindless savages again. I've never felt so out of control and yet in control at the same time before. I think if I asked Carson to get me the moon, he would. I also think if I asked him to feed me cake and tell me I'm pretty, he would.

And I know he'd fuck me until I couldn't move if I wanted him to.

"Say what's on your mind." He stands slowly, never breaking eye contact with me.

"I'm trying to figure out what I want." That confession goes miles deeper than he'll probably take it.

"Take your time deciding. I'm not going anywhere." He prowls around me, trailing a featherlight touch across my belly. Once behind me, he kisses the back of my shoulder and presses his dick against the top of my ass. It's like hot steel on my skin.

My eyes flutter shut when he nips my neck and runs his hands up and down my ribcage. I feel like a goddess in the palm of a god. I trust this man way more than I should, considering he's still a stranger to me. Why does he feel so safe? So good?

So perfect?

Because he is.

He's shown me more than once that I hold the power here and is letting me experiment and explore at my own pace. If only I could slow the hell down for a minute.

But I don't want to. What we did outside was amazing. I want to do it again. Now that I understand what happened, and why I had those extreme emotions, I'm not afraid of it anymore.

I feel like a live wire just thinking about how explosive we could get with each other.

"You look like you've just figured out what you want." Carson drags a hand through his hair and waits.

"I want you to…" I'm jumping off the deep end here. "Fuck my ass."

He goes still. I notice his Adam's apple bob when he swallows. "You sure?"

"I wouldn't say it if I wasn't." Feeling a little ashamed, I tuck my hair behind my ears and look down.

Carson wasn't having that. He tips my chin up with his finger and locks his gaze with mine. "Tell me where your mind just went."

I don't want to. But I will because I promised him honesty. "I feel embarrassed asking for it."

"Why?"

"My last partner didn't like the same things I did. He… Well, I like it rough. I want to feel trapped and be used. He—" Why am I bringing him up at a time like this? "He said it was just a phase. That I'd read too many romance novels, and I'd filled my head with unrealistic expectations. When we tried anal sex, it hurt, and he just kept saying that he was giving me what I wanted and that it should hurt and then got mad at me for crying about it."

Carson's expression morphs from calm, to fierce, to murderous. He scrubs his face with both hands and turns away from me.

I don't want this to derail our night. I shouldn't have said anything at all. "Cars—"

"Thank you for telling me." He rubs his hands on his thighs before turning to face me again. "Any negativity you have in your mind about sex or 'unrealistic expectations', I want to know about, okay? Always. This dynamic won't work unless we're on the same page. I may be able to read your body, but I can't read your mind."

"I feel terrible bringing this up right now." Looking around his room, guilt drowns me because I've just ruined our night again. "I'm so sorry."

"Don't be."

"But this just derailed us."

"No, it hasn't." He takes my hand and kisses it. "We're right on track, Mak. And there are ways to make it hurt less, and maybe not even hurt at all."

I believe him. "Good. Because I still really want to try this with you." My heart skitters around my chest. "I'll say Cupcake if it's too much." Lord knows this man has the control and precision of a machine. He's been able to stop on a dime more than once, even when he was likely seconds away from his release.

"If we do this, Mak, you know I can't come down your throat."

"I know." As if voicing a fear of mine made room for more confidence to fill its place. "There's more than one way my body can swallow you."

"Fuuuuck, you say the most perfect things." Cupping my cheek, he kisses me slowly, sensually, and it gets me all hot and bothered again. After pulling away, he runs his thumb across my mouth and growls.

Holy shit, that's so hot.

"Get on the bed and lie on your side for me, little vixen."

I do as he asks, overthinking it every step of the way. Once I'm in position, I want to curl up and die a little. This doesn't feel sexy at all. I can't believe I blurted out that I wanted anal like that. And I can't believe he's so willing to give me what I want, no matter what it is.

As I stare at the wall of floggers, crops, cuffs and rope, running through every situation in my head about how this might go, Carson gets something out of his bedside table drawer. When he lays down behind me, I hear the top of a container pop open loudly in the otherwise silent room. Distracting myself from what we're about to attempt, I keep staring at his wall of toys and imagine what it would be like getting flogged while restrained. Bet it would be nice. Or would it be terrifying?

Sweet fuckery, all of this feels scary. I'm back to being in way over my head.

What was I thinking? Carson's a professional Dom and I'm too new for him. He's going to get sick of me. He's expert level and I'm only a beginner, which makes me want to prove that I can do things I'm scared of, and I'll end up disappointing us both if I don't slow down.

The bed dips down behind me.

Oh shit, oh shit, oh shit.

This man's dick is big. Not over the top donkey-sized, but large enough to catch your attention and keep it for a long time. My pussy aches from it and we barely fucked. What will my ass feel like once this is over?

Okay, maybe I shouldn't try this. Maybe I should—

Carson spoons me and places one hand on my hip to hold me. Rubbing his thumb along my side, he says, "I'm going to slip my finger inside you, okay?"

I nod.

"Use your words, Mak. I can't do this until I hear you say yes or no."

"Yes." I brace myself and hold my breath. A finger won't be bad. I've done that before.

"You'll feel some pressure, but it shouldn't hurt. If it does, tell me."

"Okay."

The pad of his finger presses against my asshole. I expect him to shove it inside, but he doesn't. Instead, Carson rubs small circles around, which feels soft and wet and strange.

"That's a good girl." He kisses the back of my shoulder. "Just like that."

I realize I'm wiggling my ass against his finger. Then it slips in. The pressure isn't terrible. In fact, I want a little more. Tipping my head back against him, I tell him exactly that.

"More you want, more you get, but let's go slow." His finger slips in a little deeper. Then he slides it out and pushes it back in, twisting it while he works me open. "You're doing really well, Mak."

His praise makes me bolder. "More. I want

a second finger."

He nips my shoulder blade and my pussy and ass both clench from it. The sensation makes me grunt shamelessly.

"Easy now." He starts probing me, this time with two fingers. "That's it. You're doing so good for me."

We go slow like this until I'm about to scream. Holy fuck, I'm so riled up and sweaty and my head's starting to get a little fuzzy. I hear the lube top pop open again and it sounds like he's squirting a good amount onto his dick this time. There's a little shuffling and then I brace myself for what I fear will be the most painful sexual experience I've had in my life to date.

"What's your word, Mak?"

"Cupcake."

"Good girl." He presses the tip of his dick to my tight hole. "When you're ready, rock back into me. This happens at your pace, not mine. I'm just going to lie still and let you take the lead."

I freeze as those words sink in.

The power is mine. All I have to do is back it up. Okay, I've got this.

Wiggling my bottom against his dick, the air whooshes out of me. We're both so slick and when I press back against him a little harder, the pressure feels unreal when his head starts to push into my puckered hole.

"Nice and slow," he says calmly. "Take

your time."

I feel buzzy and giddy and scared. Gulping, I clench the bed sheets and wiggle a little more. I know if I can just get his head past the tight ring of muscle, I'll have a chance at actually fulfilling another one of my fantasies.

"Now use this," he says, handing me a flexible circular thing. "It's a cock ring with a vibrator on top." He presses the side and turns it on. "Hold it against on your clit."

"Okay." I'm all too relieved for the extra stimulation, if only to distract me from what I'm trying to do.

It takes me longer than I want to admit before his head is in. Carson's freehand never leaves my hip. He just rubs slow circles along my skin, which offers a calmness to my otherwise chaotic state. I feel like I could come if I didn't have this big cock halfway out of me.

I want more. I want the whole damn thing.

Pushing back against him, Carson slides deeper inside me. Pulling out a smidge, I press back again and repeat this over and over and over. It feels good. Really fucking good. Between my ass being filled and the vibration on my clit, I'm close to having an orgasm already.

Shoving back one last time, he finally bottoms out.

"I did it." I can't believe I'm proud of myself over this, but I am.

"Good girl." He keeps his hands where

they are. "Now fuck me until you're ready for me to fuck you."

Keeping one hand on the vibrator against my clit, I finally let go of the sheets I've been clenching and blow out a long breath. "You feel so good," I whisper.

"So do you."

I slowly fuck him in this backwards-sideways awkward position until pressure builds in my pussy. Eager to chase my release, I reach down and finger myself while rocking back on Carson and still manage to keep the vibrator going strong. When I come, my inner walls spasms and his dick in my ass feels even bigger when my body grips him. Sweat trickles down my temples and back. Our body heat could melt iron. "I'm ready for you to fuck me now."

"You sure?"

"Yes." My heart's about to leap out of my chest. I'm so turned on, I feel like I'm floating again. "Yes, yes, yes."

Carson is balls deep inside me when he rolls us over so I'm on my belly. "Lift your sweet ass up for me."

I press my knees together and pop my butt up as much as I can. Carson's forearms bracket my shoulders, his fists digging into the mattress by my face. I feel contained while my mind is nothing but chaos.

"That's a good girl. You're taking this cock

so well, little vixen." Growling in my ear, he moves slowly at first, hitting some part deep inside me that has me gasping. Goosebumps erupt on my arms and legs. My nipples harden into pebbles. When he bites my shoulder, I beg for him to fuck me faster. Before long, our bodies are slapping together, and I can barely breathe past the onslaught of sensations wracking through me. "I'm gonna come in this tight little ass."

"Yes, please. Give me everything you've got." I wish I could turn around to see his expression, but I can't with how I'm pinned.

"You want my cum in your ass, don't you?"

"Yes."

"I'm going to fill you up and watch it drip out."

He pumps in and out of me while I hold on to his forearms to keep from rocking too hard. Carson's thighs shake when he comes inside me, and I swear his dick gets bigger while this happens. I feel it jerk. Hearing him roar with his climax, I turn into a puddle on his bed. I'm hot but shivering. Breathless but breathing.

He peppers my back with soft kisses and slowly pulls out of me. The moment our bodies separate, I cringe.

"Stay still." He bites my butt cheek playfully before hopping off the bed. Turning my face in his direction, I watch him saunter into his bathroom. Damn, his ass is juicy. I want to bite him like a peach. The faucet turns on and a moment later, he comes back out with a towel. "It's warm, so it won't be too uncomfortable."

I lay there like a lump while he cleans me up. I don't even have the nerve to ask how big of a mess there is back there, or what kind. Honestly, I don't even care. He's done this more than me, so he knew what to expect and how to handle it.

"Thank you," I blink up at him. "For not making it hurt."

"Thank you for trusting me to give you a good experience."

Is it weird that we're being appreciative? I don't know and I don't care. This was a good night and I'm really happy.

Carson goes back into the bathroom and doesn't come back out for a few minutes. It's all the time it takes for me to succumb to exhaustion. When he steps back out, he smiles warmly and climbs back into the bed. "Come here." Spooning me again, he grabs the bedspread and folds it over us so we're in a burrito. I melt in his arms, too tired to budge. "Want me to run you a bath?"

"No."

"Need cookies? Water?"

"No."

"What can I do for you, Mak? You have to tell me."

"Just hold me for a little?"

"I plan to hold you all night." He kisses the top of my head, and it makes me feel precious. "You can stay, right?"

I wasn't planning to, but now that I'm here, I can't bring myself to leave yet. My eyes are already so heavy. I don't think I have any bones left in my body.

"You did amazing, Mak. That was a lot for one go, and you blew my mind with how well you took me."

I'm too tired to respond.

Chapter 13

Carson

I wake up the next morning blindly reaching out for Mak. My stomach drops when I realize she's not there. Then I hear shuffling by the door and crack my eyes open to see her staring at the wall of toys I have hanging on display. "See something you like?"

Her fingers comb through a flogger that's on the tamer side. "You use all these?" There's no judgment in her tone.

"If my partner wants me to, I will. And sometimes I also like to be on the receiving end." Mak is wrapped in my bedspread and holds it close to her chest. I want nothing more than to rip it off her body and have her as my breakfast in bed. "If there's anything you're curious about, let me know and I'll explain. Or show you. They look scarier than they really are."

She touches a cat o' nine tails that has beads on the end. "This looks painful."

"Depends on your threshold." Sitting up, I yawn and stretch my arms until something in my shoulder pops. Man, that felt good. "Do you have to go to work?"

"Umm." She scratches her head. Her hair looks knotty and frizzy, and I want to gather it in my hands and pull it. "I don't have to go in until three today."

It just occurred to me that I have no clue what this woman does for a living. "Hungry?"

Sliding out of the bed, my morning wood is on full display as I pull out a fresh pair of boxers from my dresser. After Mak fell asleep last night, I was still too restless to join her, and spent the better part of three hours watching her facial expressions, counting her breaths, swiping the hair from her face, and making sure she was all tucked in tight regardless of how much she tossed and turned. Then I went downstairs to edit some more photos and sent them off to my clients in their passcode protected galleries. After that, I lifted weights in my garage and took a shower.

Since it's just after seven in the morning, I've gotten about two and a half hours of sleep. I can work with that. "We need coffee and waffles."

"No coffee for me. I'm a tea girl."

"And here I thought you were perfect."

"I am." She grins. "You're the one with beverage issues."

I growl at her in a playful way and love how her breath catches.

Before I have a chance to drop to my knees

and worship her pussy, Mak looks around my room in confusion. "Where did I leave my clothes?"

Something in me panics. I don't want her to get dressed yet. But I also want her comfortable and warm. My little vixen has goosebumps all over her arms. *Shit*. I run hot and keep my house on the cool side all year round. The fire downstairs definitely died out by now, so it's a little chillier than usual in here. I quickly grab a hoodie from my closet and toss it to her. "Put this on."

Mak bites her lip, but does as I command. I like that she listens so well. I don't have the patience to tame a brat—not that they could be tamed anyway—but they're just not my type.

I catch her inhaling the fabric of the hoodie and pretend I didn't see it happen. "Are you sore?"

"A little." She plays with the hoodie strings. "It's oddly kind of nice."

That's good. I hope her experience last night was a great one for her. I plan to give her many more.

My black hoodie hits her knees. Did she shrink in the middle of the night? I swear every time I look at her from a different angle, she's smaller and more mesmerizing.

I want to devour her. Bet she tastes sweet as candy first thing in the morning. "How's your headspace?"

"Good." She gathers her knotty hair and lets it fall over her shoulders, then puts the hood up over her head. "I feel strange, but it's nice. I'm all loose and calm inside."

Hopefully she stays that way. I'm not cocky enough to say I fucked her boneless, because last night I barely did a thing, but I'm glad she's in a good spot mentally and physically today. As her Dom, it's my job to make sure she's steady and safe, even after a scene ends. The adrenaline she felt last night in the yard wasn't the same as what flooded her system in my bed. One was fear and excitement. The other was cautious experimentation.

She fucked me, not the other way around. Even when I was on top, Mak still set the pace and drove my actions, regardless of whether she realized it or not.

Going off her body language last night, I think it's safe to say she thought I was just going to ram her ass with my dick. Mak braced herself to let me do just that, which made me feel extra protective of her. I can't erase what her ex did to destroy her first time with anal, but I can make it better for her from here on out.

In this dynamic, I give her control, patience, and encouragement. She gifts me her body, trust, and submission.

Just thinking about how good it was coming inside her tight little ass has me dying to do it again.

"Come on." I playfully tug her hair and head out of the bedroom first. If I stay in here while she's looking this adorable, I'll fuck her until she can't walk away from me.

The first thing I notice when I hit the bottom step is the familiar sound of scratching at my sliding back door. *Damnit, Cooper.* I storm over and open the damned thing to let the dog in.

"I didn't know you had a dog!" Mak drops to her knees when the goofy animal runs right to her, wagging his tail because he's an attention whore.

"He's the neighbor's and gets out all the time. They have the farm next door."

"Aww, you're so cute!" Mak giggles as the chocolate lab jumps up and knocks her over. "Omph!"

"Cooper, down!" I grab him by the collar and pull him off her. "No jumping." Cooper sits, still wagging his tail hard enough to make his entire back half sway across my floor. Reaching out for Mak's hand, I help pull her up. "You okay? He didn't hurt you, did he?"

"I'm fine." She bends down and starts scratching Cooper's ears. "He's such a lovey!"

"He's a sucker for pretty girls."

"You have that in common."

Touché. I toss her an easy smile before making my way into the kitchen to start breakfast. Mak follows me and, of course,

Cooper follows her. Filling my kettle up with water, I yawn before putting it on the stove to boil. Then I grab the waffle mix from my pantry and a bowl.

Mak sits at my table as if she's lived here her whole life. Cooper lays by her feet like this is his home too. For a second, I'm awestruck by the situation. It's easy with Mak. Fun and simple. I want to feed her and take care of her and protect her and—

Whoa. Nope.

Jesus Christ, the woman's a witch and I'm under her spell. It's the only thing that makes sense because where my thought train just took me was nowhere near where I've wanted to go in a very long time.

"Do you have any photoshoots today?"

I blink, snapping out of my mini panic attack and snag a box of black tea from the back of my cupboard. Ripping the package open with my teeth, I drop the sachet into a mug and then get coffee going for myself with my French press. "No boudoir shoots, but I do have other appointments."

"Oh." Mak's knee starts bobbing. I wonder if she's nervous or impatient to leave.

"What do you do for a living?"

"Um. I'm a hospice nurse."

I nearly drop my bag of coffee. "Really? That sounds…" *Sad, hard, scary, depressing…* "Interesting."

I suck at small talk.

"I love it." Mak's eyes round like she said something she shouldn't have. "I mean, it's sad and hard sometimes, but it's also really rewarding. I'm not scared of death, and this job makes me feel like I'm making a difference when I'm with someone during their last days. I've been with some of my patients for a couple years before they'd pass. Others, just a few days. It's all different, and somehow all the same. It's hard to explain."

I listen quietly and pour batter into the waffle maker.

"I feel bad for some of them. They don't have anyone, and I think it's tough for them to be lonely in the end. But we all die alone, right? Unless you're in a plane crash or something like that, but also it kind of sucks to take your last breath with no one there to keep you company. But I've had some people ask for everyone to leave because they didn't want anyone with them. It's their call, obviously, but sometimes it's good to just, I don't know, sit with them in silence. Give them peaceful vibes until they're gone."

I nod because I don't know how else to respond.

"Some of them have a lot of family that gather around. That's beautiful too. And sad. I guess I was made without the emotion you're supposed to feel when someone dies, because it's never really bothered me. Not that I've had to live through someone close to me passing away yet, but being around it everyday kind of dulls the heartache of it, I guess."

I think she talks a lot when she's nervous.

"I feel bad for the spouses. It must be devastating to lose a soul mate."

"I'm sure." Flipping the waffle maker open to pluck out the first golden brown circle, I plop it on a plate. "At least they had time to spend together."

"Yeah," she sighs. "I've never been much for marriage or babies or anything, but I wouldn't mind spending my life with someone. I think it would be nice to find my penguin."

I grab syrup from my fridge and have a death grip on it and the plate of waffles. Placing both in front of her, I cautiously ask, "You don't want marriage or kids?"

My heart holds its fucking breath while I wait for her answer.

"No. I don't."

I can't, for the life of me, make the right set of words come out of my mouth.

She crosses her arms protectively around herself and glares up at me with worry in her gaze. Even Cooper must sense her attitude's changed because he perks up from under the table. "Is that something you want?"

We're going for the kill shot here.

"No," I say firmly. "Those things are not

for me." I've never wanted to get married and I sure as fuck don't want kids. Those things are great for other people, I just don't have any interest. But I never expected Mak to be on the same page as me about it.

She blows out a loud breath and her shoulders sag. "That's a relief." She stiffens again. "I mean kudos to people who want those things. It's just not for me. I never understood the point of marriage and I definitely have zero desire for kids."

I bite back my smile and make another waffle. This woman is too perfect for me. Glancing over my shoulder at her, I spill a secret not many of my subs know. "I had a vasectomy when I was twenty-three."

Her jaw drops a little, but she quickly recovers. "That's... really convenient. I've been on birth control for forever and hate it."

If this leads to a long-term thing, she can stop taking those meds if she wants, but that'll be her decision.

"Can I ask you a question, Carson?"

"Ask away." I keep my back to her and focus on making breakfast. Steam billows out of the waffle maker and my hands are shaking a little.

"Why'd you take your snakebites out?"

The question catches me off guard. "How'd you know about those?"

"I saw them in your profile pic on

K!nkLink. Very emo with the black hair, by the way."

Shit, I forgot about my profile pic. That was an old one that I haven't updated in a while. I cut my natural black hair about four inches shorter since then and regret it often. "I took all my piercings out about a month ago. No reason why, just wanted a change, I guess." After plating my stack of waffles, I sit across from her and notice she hasn't touched her breakfast yet. "Eat before it gets cold."

"Do you have chocolate syrup?"

I'm midway pouring maple syrup on my waffles when I stop what I'm doing and grab her what she needs from the fridge. "Sugar junkie, huh?"

"Chocolate junkie." She drizzles an obscene amount all over her plate until each square is filled with it. "Don't judge me."

"I would never." We eat in silence for a few moments and then I sit back and take a sip of my coffee that's finally ready.

Mak pours chocolate into her tea too—I have no words. Instead of asking for something else, she pops up and goes to my fridge for the milk and pours that in her cup as well. "Do you have any cinnamon?"

"Second cabinet to the left of the fridge."

"Found it! Thanks." She sprinkles that into her tea too.

"What kind of witch's brew are you

making, woman?"

"Ha! I can't share ancient secrets with mere mortals." Mak plops back down and pulls the hood off her head. "Too bad you don't have any frog's breath."

I narrow my gaze at her. "There's nothing more suspicious than frog's breath."

She bursts out laughing and almost spills her drink. "You can't be more perfect, Carson."

I salute her with my mug and take another sip. Only the elite know lines from great movies like *The Nightmare Before Christmas*.

"So, what got you into hospice care?"

She curls up on her chair and digs into her waffle. "I just fell into it. I always wanted to be in healthcare, but I didn't know what field. This one popped up and I loved it. End of story."

We take our time eating and chatting. The sun shines through my kitchen window and hits Mak's head, showing that her dark brown hair has shots of copper running through it. Man, she's gorgeous.

And way out of my league.

She finishes her breakfast and takes her plate to the sink, grabbing mine too when she passes me. I try to stop her. "I've got it."

"No, no. You cooked. I'll clean."

She washes my dishes, and I'm at a complete loss for words. Mak acts like she lives here. Why do I like it so much?

I'm a territorial man. I don't like people

touching me or my things. I rarely bring lovers home and all that fun stuff upstairs rarely gets used anymore. I keep it all on display for myself because I like them and they cost a lot of money to have custom made, so I don't want them just sitting in a box, hidden and unnoticed. In fact, I haven't used any of those things since—

Stop it.

Snagging my coffee mug, I chug the rest. I refuse to go down rabbit holes that will take me months to climb out of again.

Mak cleans the plates and puts them on the drying rack while I watch her like a predator. Her legs are so dainty. Her feet are bare and toes unpainted. I like how simple she is. Even with the leftover makeup and smudged mascara, Mak is a wet dream. I want to wash all that residual makeup off her face so I can see the real woman under the foundation and highlighter and whatever other shit Chloe put on her face yesterday.

"Shower with me." I don't make it a question, but she has every right to deny me.

"I..." Mak licks her lips, her gaze swinging to the clock on my microwave. "Okay."

Triumph has me out of my chair and on her in an instant. I pick her up, intending to carry her all the way to my bathroom upstairs. I like that I can grab her like this. I like that she lets me. I could toss her into the air and catch her with ease.

Hey, I might not look like a chiseled body builder, but I'm strong as fuck. I just can't ever get rid of the extra cushion around my middle.

If dad bods have a boss level, I've reached it.

Mak's got her legs wrapped around me again, and I wonder if I'm too thick for her to hook her ankles around my back. Holding her ass in my hands, I feel like a dragon hording his treasure. She kisses me while I'm still going up the steps and I almost trip and drop her. "Shit."

Mak giggles as if she loves the fact that I stumbled from being too distracted with her mouth on mine.

Growling playfully, I get us the rest of the way to my bathroom and prop her on the counter. "Stay." I back away to start the shower. "Hot, cold, or warm?"

Mak's eyebrows raise to her hairline. "I don't care."

"You have to care. Everyone cares." It pisses me off that I don't know the answer to this already. There are a billion things I don't know about Mak, and it makes me feel useless.

"As hot as you can stand it."

"Good girl." I want her to tell me exactly what she wants, what she likes, what she needs. The fact that she's taken my personal preference into account with this makes me happy too. I tap the faucet and make it a little hotter than I can handle, only because I usually take lukewarm showers. Hey, I wasn't kidding when I said I run hot. My body temp is high all the time and there are days I take ice cold showers to cool down after a workout.

Returning to Mak, I lift my hoodie off her body in one swift tug. Her tight, tiny tits are the first thing I see, and I watch her nipples harden from the chilly air. The shower can wait. I want to taste her first. Spreading her legs, I squat down to lick her pussy.

She moans.

That's all I need to hear before I'm thoroughly eating her cunt like a starved man at a banquet. She's tart and sweet on my tongue. I want to know what she would taste like with my cum dripping out of her. "I want to fuck you before we get wet."

Shower sex sucks, in my opinion. Water isn't lube, it just makes things uncomfortable and the steam fucks with my senses.

Mak's hooded gaze sets me on fire. "Make me come first, then fuck me and make me come again."

Her demands momentarily stun me. With her perfect little pussy in my face, I have to wonder where this woman came from. Why has it taken so long for her to come into my life? "Yes ma'am."

She giggles just before making the most undignified groan when I shove two fingers inside her cunt and hit her g-spot. It's not hard to find, and once I do, I nail it over and over while sucking on her clit.

"Holy shit, Carson." She digs her hands into my hair and holds my face where she wants it. I love that she's so confident. I love that when she knows what she wants, she's not afraid to get it.

I'm relentless in my pursuit of her first orgasm of the day. I want it to be a big one.

"Don't stop. Oh my God, please don't stop. Right there." Her thighs clamp around my head like earmuffs. "I'm coming... oh fuck, I'm coming!"

That she does. Her body spasms, inner walls clamping down on my fingers while I stimulate her clit in short little sucks with my mouth. My girl detonates and screams for all she's worth.

I've never been more appreciative of acoustics in a bathroom before.

Standing up, I jerk her forward so she's half-dangling on my countertop and thrust my dick into her. "Your pussy is so swollen and needy for me."

"Mmmph." She digs her nails into my shoulders. "Fuck, you feel so good in me."

I rail her hard and fast, our skin slapping in the steamy bathroom, until our breaths turn ragged. Then I slow my pace and take my time with her while my orgasm builds. Rubbing her clit with the pad of my thumb, I feel her inner walls squeeze me. "That's it. Come on my cock for me. I want your body to clamp down on my dick."

Her jaw drops in a silent scream. Mak's eyes lock onto mine and I swear I fall into some kind of abyss. My balls draw in tight, and I explode. "That's a good girl. Take everything I give you." I thrust into her slowly, unloading my cum until I can't stand how sensitive my cock becomes. Pulling out, I look down and say, "Push it out."

My girl obeys beautifully.

When my cum drips out of her pussy, I gather some of it on my fingers and shove them into her mouth. Leaning in with a growl, I kiss her so we can taste what we're like together.

Fuck, this woman is magic. Pulling away, I admire how flushed her cheeks are. How big her pupils have become. "Can you stand?"

"Yes," she says, playfully smacking my chest.

It's disappointing to see she's not lying when she hops off my sink and lands solidly on her feet.

I'll have to try harder next time.

Chapter 14

Mak

What the hell am I doing? I need to get out of here, and yet there's no part of me that wants to leave. Now I'm about to take a shower with Carson when I should be going home and getting myself together for work, run errands, and call Leah to tell her *everything*.

But there's no way I'm leaving just yet. I'm having way too much fun and hellooooo, Carson in jeans and a t-shirt is sinful, but Carson naked and wet?

My pussy is quivering.

No lie. This man is hot with a capital F-U-C-K-M-E-P-L-E-A-S-E.

I can't believe how hot morning sex is with this man. It's dirty and slow and intense and… addictive.

Boneless, I step into his shower first and sigh when the spray hits my back with gloriously hot water.

Carson steps in with me and watches with hungry eyes.

Saturating my hair, I feel different and can't pinpoint how.

"Here." He holds a bottle of shampoo and squirts some into my palm. I didn't expect him to wash my hair for me, but just this little bit of attention stirs something warm in my belly. I swear Carson's constantly trying to provide in some way. In the boudoir shoot, it was encouragement. At the bar, it was protection. In the back woods, it was excitement. In the bed, it was safety and reassurance.

The last bit is almost laughable. I felt safe getting fucked in the ass. That doesn't make sense, but it's the only way my mind can categorize it. He let me fuck him, let me set the pace, let me call the shots, and that's honestly not something I've had before with a lover. He turned a bad first time into an amazing second chance and now I can't wait to try it again.

Carson seems very aware of his size and is careful not to elbow me in the head or step on my toes as we maneuver around each other in the small shower. He's not the largest man I've ever been with, but he's also not the smallest. He's the perfect size.

For me.

As I finish rinsing, my heart starts pounding. We aren't saying a word to each other, and I can't tell if I like the silence or not. I don't know what to say. Maybe he doesn't either. Or maybe he likes quiet in the mornings. I wish there was music playing. Okay, I'll just hurry up and finish in here, then get out.

Chill, Mak. Not every exchange has to be filled with noise…

"Stay here for a minute," Carson orders. He steps out of the shower first while I remain under the hot spray until he pulls the curtain open. He's got a towel around his waist, one tossed over his shoulder, and is holding another out for me. I turn the water off and step out to let him wrap me up, laughing when he drops the second towel on my head and dries my hair in the worst way. "Stop! You'll get me all tangled up!"

Lifting the towel off my head, he steals a kiss and we both start laughing.

After getting dressed, he insists I wear his hoodie home. We make small talk because I'm honestly dragging my feet, and finally we kiss goodbye.

Once I get in my car, Carson waves me off and shuts his front door. My heart skitters in my chest. I don't want to leave. I miss him already and that is seriously so fucking stupid.

Holy shit, what's wrong with me?

I'm so mixed up about this entire twenty-four hours, it almost scares me. Pulling out of the driveway like a bat out of Hell, I force myself to not look back.

• • •

"It's just good dick," Leah says on the

phone call home.

"Yeah, but I've had good dick before. Carson's different."

"Do not tell me you fell in love in one night, Mak truck. That's too fast, even for you."

"Hell no." I'm half-laughing, half-cringing. "I think this must be the lingering aftereffects of my sub drop last night." At least, I hope that's what this is, because I honestly feel attached to this man and that's not okay. He'll think I'm psycho for getting clingy and he'll likely cut me loose and never speak to me again.

I'm not ready for our fun to end yet.

"Tell me *everything*. I want all the details."

Exhaling dramatically, I walk around the aisles at the store, dropping random shit I need into my cart. "Well..." Where to begin? "He chased me through his backyard and into the woods."

"No way! Oh, hot *and* creepy. Stalker fetish much?"

"It's primal, not stalker. More like he's the predator and I'm the prey." Now that I think about it, I guess stalker and primal could kind of go together. "It was exciting and a little terrifying."

"Did he fuck you in the dirt with twigs snapping against your spine?"

"No, he went down on me." I skip the details of how he basically covered half his face with my arousal. Holy wow, thinking about it now has me dying to watch him do that again.

"And how was his tongue game?"

"The best I've ever had." I toss a bag of chips into my cart. "Like the *best*, Leah. If my clit was a bullseye, he hit the target on the first flick and was relentless until he had me screaming his name to the damn moon."

"Ahhh, it's so refreshing when someone knows how to be efficient and precise."

"Totally." I turn my cart into the next aisle, barely remembering all the things I'm here for. Damnit, I'll have to make a second round through this whole ass store because I've absentmindedly passed half of what's on my list already. "Then we did anal."

I smile at an older woman who's left her cart in the middle of the aisleway. Trying, and failing, to scooch past her, she just glares at me struggling with my cart, so I glower right back.

Rude.

"No way!" Leah screams into my earbuds. "You said you'd never do butt stuff again."

"Well never say never, right? But he didn't fuck me in the ass. *I* basically fucked *him* with my ass. It was amazing." I move the woman's cart out of my damn way and shoot her another toothy smile. "Then he took over once I was ready, and I swear I didn't know orgasms like that existed."

"Can you sit?"

"Yeah. Surprisingly." Carson's not walking

around with a twelve-inch pipe between his legs, but it's still long and thick enough to fuck me up if he wanted it to. "Oh, and he has a *ton* of BDSM toys. Leah, I shit you not, I stalled out for a second when I went into his bedroom. He must have a dozen different floggers and cuffs hanging on his wall."

"Does he have a brother? Do you guys want a third? I'll be your third, baby. I'll fuck you so well, you won't even remember Carson's there."

I burst out laughing and walk aimlessly through the next aisle. Wait. Crap! I'm in the car maintenance section. How the hell did I get here? Next, I hit the kid's toy section. I'm seriously wasting so much time, but I don't care. I feel too happy to care. Last night might have been the best night of my life. "He's seriously nothing like I thought he'd be."

"You should have known better than to go in with expectations, Mak. But I'm glad he exceeds them. You deserve to be treated like a goddess, and it sounds like he might be the one to worship you properly."

"Well, I definitely feel worshipped that's for sure. He kept trying to take care of me, even in tiny ways. When I dropped the first time after the woods thing, he switched gears so fast and before I could get a grip, he had me wrapped in blankets on his couch, had a fire stoked to warm me up, and fed me cookies."

"I hate you." Leah sighs, dreamily. "You have all the luck. My hookup last night had a crooked dick, zero knowledge of how to use it to my advantage and didn't even *try* to find my clit. He was a great kisser, just not great at much else. It was like being railed by a bunny. Lasted about as long as one too. Ugh, so depressing."

"Boo. Bad dick downs are worse than no dick downs." I turn into the next aisle and my cart slams into someone else's. "I'm so sorry!" I rush to say before looking up.

Fuck. My. Life.

"Hey, Mak."

"Who's that?" Leah growls in my earbuds.

"I..." My face grows hot with embarrassment. "Hey."

He-who-was-awful-at-dickdowns beams me a big smile. "I was just thinking about you."

Liar.

"Mind if I stop by later today and pick up the rest of my stuff?"

Words form on my tongue, but my mouth just opens and closes like I've turned into a goldfish. Leah yells profanities in my ear because she realizes who I've run into, and I can't string my thoughts together fast enough to make a decent snarky refusal.

"I can drop by after eight, if that works for you."

"No, sorry." Thank God I manage to rub two brain cells together. "I got rid of all your shit."

He's mad. His face always looks extra dumb when he's angry. "What the hell, Mak? I said I would get it when I had the time."

"But you never did. You just kept stringing me along about it and I told you I'm not a storage facility."

I can tell he wants to yell at me, but doesn't want to make a scene. Instead, he shakes his head like he's super disappointed in my behavior. "That really sucks, Makayla. You know I've been collecting that stuff for years. Even before we got together. You know that collection was important to me."

Guilt creeps in.

"Don't you dare let him gaslight you, Mak. Fuck that trashy asshole."

I've never been more grateful to have Leah on the phone than I am right now. Rolling my shoulders back, I look him straight in the eye and say, "If it was so important to you, you would have picked it all up months ago. I gave you plenty of chances, and you didn't take a single one." That goes for not just the glass collection, but everything in our relationship. "Snooze you lose, asshole."

I shove my cart down the aisle and walk faster to get out of there.

He doesn't follow. I didn't expect him to, but a little piece of me is still worried he might try to chase me down in the parking lot or something.

"I'm so proud of you girl." Leah's voice sounds wonky in my ears. "You did great."

It doesn't feel that way. Guilt eats me up because maybe I should have texted him one last time to say if he didn't get his stuff by the end of the day that I was going to destroy it. Or I could have just dropped it off at his house for him. Instead, I was vindictive and smashed his collection of glasses because I wanted to feel cathartic.

I was selfish and now I feel awful about it.

"Don't you dare feel bad about smashing his shit," Leah growls in my ear.

"I don't."

"Liar. I can practically feel your energy through the phone. You've gone all quiet and you, Mak, are anything but quiet. Don't let him guilt you into thinking you're the bad guy here. It's glasses, for fuck's sake. He'll get over it."

"Yeah." I don't have the energy to put any oomph in my response. "Listen, I gotta go check out now and don't want to be rude to the cashier. I'll call you later."

"Okay. Love you, bye."

"Love you too, bye."

I'm not calling her back. I doubt I'll be doing anything for the rest of the day until I have to go to work.

Mak: zero.

He-who-is-a-prick: one.

Chapter 15

Carson

"Bend your right leg and extend the left one behind you. Good, now place your hand on the arm of the couch. Juuust like that. Now push your butt out and arch your back. Little more. That's it." I snap a half dozen pictures before coming over to my client. "Can I fix your hair real quick?"

"Sure."

"Okay, hold still." I fluff her long black hair out and let more of it fall over her shoulder. "Alright, look back over at me again aaaand..." *Click, click, click.* "Perrrrfect. You're a natural, Magan."

"You just make this easy. My cousin said you were the best, and she was right."

"You haven't seen the final pics yet."

"Don't need to. This experience alone has been so rewarding. Five stars. Highly recommend."

"Well thanks." I take a few more pictures before directing her into a new position. My cell vibrates in my pocket and the urge to see if it's

Mak is strong, but I clamp down on my resolve and stay focused on my client instead.

After Mak left my house three days ago, she hasn't tried to contact me. I feel sick about it. I think I've fucked up somehow and don't know how to fix it. Her silence confuses me. She seemed happy and sated when she left the next morning, and I told her to call me when she had free time. I don't know what made me think she'd call me that night.

Lame, I know. I should just call her, but I want Mak to have control here. I'll come when she beckons—trust me. I'd told her that if I'm going to be the one who controls how our scenes are, I wanted her to be the one to initiate contact first. At least in the beginning.

I'm still worried I went too fast and hard on her the other night. The last thing I want to do is scare her away.

My cell buzzes again.

It's hard to ignore, but I'm not taking away attention from my client. Especially since she's lying upside down with her feet up in the air. "Nice. Stay just like that." I snap a few more pics until I see her face turning red. "We're done. Need help up?"

"Nope!" Magan flips over and blows out a deep sigh. "Woo. That was a head rush." She points at the sex swing. "Can I take some on that next?"

"We'll get there." I double-check the

lighting with my sensor. "I want to do some of you walking towards the window first. The light's perfect for it right now."

"Okay."

The rest of the session goes smoothly and by the end of the workday, I'm tired. I still haven't slept. I can't seem to turn my mind off long enough to get any rest and spent all night playing video games and editing Mak's photos.

They're spectacular, by the way, as I knew they would be.

After closing the studio, I finally bite the bullet and check my phone, zeroing in on two numbers: Trey's and Mak's.

Relief and dread war in my chest because all I can see of Mak's text on my notifications is "Hey, it's Mak, I..."

I hit Trey's text first because I'm a chickenshit.

Trey: Hey man. I need a fantasy shot with a woman and water elements. Something that says, "special chosen one". No price limit set. If you don't have an image already, the author is willing to pay for model and time.

Carson: I don't have any that are licensed for commercial, but I'll do a model call and find someone. Free to be creative with this?

Three little dots appear immediately. Damn, he must have been sitting on his phone.

Trey: Absolutely. She says to think High Fae Court meets Florence and the Machine.

I've got the perfect idea already.

Carson: Give me a couple weeks to set up the shoot. I'll send you samples.

Trey: You're a god. Thanks.

Carson: Bow to me.

Trey: You wish. *middle finger emoji*

Carson: Got two of those fingers? Shove them up your ass and twiddle them.

Trey: How about I shove them up yours? Nm. You'd enjoy it too much.

That makes me laugh.

Trey: You getting back online tonight?

Carson: To kick your ass? I know you like being my bitch, but you don't have to beg like this, baby.

Trey: Cool. I'll see if Glitch and Ara can join at 8. Thanks again, man. This author is a big one for me.

Carson: Np

I finally get the balls to pull up Mak's text.

Mak: Hey, it's Mak, I was wondering when you can meet up again.

My brows dig down. This feels odd. Maybe I'm just reading into it, but the text feels off to me. It's hard to read tones in a text, but this one is giving stiff vibes to me. I don't like it. So, I mirror it.

Carson: Let me know when you're free and we'll work something out.

I want to ask how she's doing. I want to see how her day went. I want to know why it's taken her three goddamn days to contact me, but that's ridiculous. I've gone weeks without talking to a sub with no issue. So why would Mak be different?

Carson: I have your photos ready btw.

Great. I can't seem to shut the fuck up.

Little bubbles appear as she types me back. I'd be a liar to say I don't have my phone in a chokehold as I wait for her reply.

Mak: Yay! I can't wait to see them!

My smile hurts my cheeks.

Carson: Come over tonight if you want.

I'm going to send her the gallery through email no matter what, but this is a natural way to open my door for her again sooner.

Mak: You sure? I don't want to intrude if you have other plans.

It's Friday night and I have no plans other than gaming at eight, which I'm not about to say because I can cancel it.

Carson: I'm heading home now. Meet you there?

It takes Mak a few minutes to read and respond to that one, which is just enough time for me to feel uneasy again.

Mak: omw

I rush out of the studio because I'm not sure how long it'll take her to get to my house, but I know I'm a good thirty minutes out, and I don't want her to wait. It's dark already and by the time I pull into my long driveway, her car is already parked.

My heart leaps into my throat. How long did she wait for me? It's freezing out and her car isn't running. When I go over to her driver's side door to open it for her, I realize she's not even in it. The fuck?

She's nowhere in sight either. It's not like she has a key to get in, so where is she?

My cell dings and I yank it out of my pocket.

Mak: Come find me.

I let out a slow exhale. Holy. Shit. This woman has no idea how much those three little words can make a man like me turn feral.

But she's about to find out.

Chapter 16

Mak

Heart in my throat, hidden in the shadows, I watch Carson read my text.

I've spent the better part of three days heavily researching primal kinks because, after the other night, I knew I needed more knowledge under my belt before I asked for another chase. A man like Carson is the perfect predator to my prey and all day long, I've been dreaming of ways to make a chase happen again.

My plan worked.

Primal play focuses on the senses: listening, scenting, and even biting, scratching, growling, and unleashing one's most carnal appetites. There can be fighting and wrestling involved as a competitive aspect for dominance and submission. It's taking what you want. There's a primitiveness to it where etiquette doesn't exist. Fuck the flowers and candles. Forget music and feathers. This is a raw, aggressive, and wild breed of desire.

I got a taste of it the other night and loved

it. Now I want the whole damn thing.

Hiding behind a tree, I watch Carson take off his shirt and toss it on the ground.

I'm only wearing his hoodie from the other day, so this is going to be fun.

My panties lay in the grass as an incentive for him. They're bright white and easy to see in the moonlight. He finds them almost immediately and when he picks them up to smell the lace—like my scent is his drug of choice and he's been dying for a hit—my pussy clenches.

I take another step back. *Snap!* A twig breaks under my heel and catches his attention.

Carson fists my panties and takes off towards where I'm currently freezing my ass off.

Game on.

I book it deeper into the woods, grateful I'm wearing running shoes. His property is basically out in the middle of nowhere and there's nothing and no one around. Not even the farmer next door is close enough to hear us, so I feel safe in letting myself go.

Carson's footsteps get louder as he swiftly approaches. I crouch behind a bush, cupping my mouth to keep from panting too loudly. I'm out of breath already and it's not from the cardio.

I'm turned on and dying for him to find me.

"Where are you, little vixen?" He growls and I'm undone. This is exhilarating and wild.

Jumping up, I take off again and squeal when Carson catches up to me. He drops me on the ground the same way he did the other night, but I'm ready this time and kick him away so I can scramble out of his reach again.

Cool air hits my bare ass when the hoodie I'm in rises up.

With another low growl, Carson grabs my ankle and slides me back. My belly scrapes across the cold, hard ground and his hand feels hot around my foot.

I kick him again, but it doesn't work a second time. He pins me to the ground with my wrists and straddles me. "Naughty girl."

Wiggling, I manage to get out of his loose grip and we wrestle across the ground together.

"Oh shit," Carson says, as if impressed by my strength.

I land on top of him, and we're both panting. Only one of us will ultimately submit, and that's going to be me. Just not yet. He better earn this pussy first.

"What's your safe word, Mak?"

"Cupcake."

"Good girl." He rolls me over and slams my arms down by my side. I groan when he digs his groin against mine. His dick is rock hard, and jeans feel rough against my bare cunt.

I shove him back and he grunts when my foot hits his pec, but I know I haven't hurt him. Instead of running, I raise onto my knees and barrel into his chest as hard as I can to knock him down.

"Oomph!" He falls backwards, taking me with him.

I had no idea wrestling half naked in the cold, dark woods would feel this amazing. I focus on getting one up on Carson by quickly snagging my panties when he accidentally drops them. Rubbing the lace obscenely between my legs, I get them good and wet before shoving them in his face to try and stuff them into his mouth.

His eyes are huge with surprise, then they narrow on me, and he growls with a mouth full of my lace. It makes me laugh. Pulling them out of his mouth, Carson keeps just the bottom part between his teeth and pulls—ripping the fabric to pieces.

Hottest. Visual. Ever.

I wish I had another pair just so he could do that trick again.

Carson shoves me back and straddles me, triumph lighting his face until I manage to twist myself out of his grip and tackle him again. We go back and forth rolling and clawing, biting and scratching each other, and I know I've gone way harder on him than he has on me. I love this. My body feels like a live wire and I'm sweating.

White puffs of air punch out of both of us as he holds me down again. I let my legs fall open to give him his prize. Carson smashes his mouth to mine and kisses me so hard, I give in completely. There's no space between our bodies for me to get his jeans unfastened. Damnit! I tap his arms and push him back.

"Have I hurt you?" he immediately asks.

"Not at all." That's when I notice metal on his mouth. "You put your piercings back in?"

His lopsided grin is adorable. "When you mentioned seeing them in my picture, it sounded like you wanted them back in."

My heart cantors in my chest. "Take your fucking pants off," I demand.

Carson stares at me for a moment, still breathing hard. Then he lifts off me and stands up. He's already shirtless and barefoot and when he finally gets naked, the hoodie I'm still in has me roasting. But I won't dare take it off. It smells like him. It feels like him. I've been wearing it for the better part of three days while I've overthought a million things.

As he drops down to straddle me again, I roll over and try to crawl away.

"Where do you think you're going?" He grabs my hips and nudges my legs open. I feel him settle behind me, then he bends all the way down and licks my pussy like it's his first meal in days.

I'm swollen with need and even I can smell myself at this point. I lift myself higher to give him better access.

"You're so fucking delicious," he growls. "I

want to gobble you up."

I remain on all fours. The entire world around me vanishes. It's just me, Carson, and a lot of heat.

"You're so wet and puffed out." His next growl makes my body melt. "My little vixen needs to get fucked, doesn't she?"

"Yes."

He pushes the tip of his cock inside me and it feels like I'm being stretched. He pushes and recedes slowly, making me take him an inch at a time.

"Stop playing nice," I beg. "I want your leash off, Carson."

A warning growl is all I get before he slams into me, bottoming out in one hard thrust.

It knocks the air from my lungs because of how deep he is. When Carson gathers my hair in his hands, he pulls it while fucking me from behind. My hoodie is stifling. I can't get it off and don't have the capacity to ask for help. Not with the way his thrusts have conquered my brain cells. He must notice what I'm trying to do and tugs me until I'm on my knees, pressed against his back. Then pulls the hoodie off for me. "Better?"

"Yes." Cool air hits my skin and I feel like I can breathe again.

Until he wraps his hand around my throat and drives into me again. My nails scrape his thighs as he wrings pleasure from my body.

I'm still reeling when he lets go of my throat and tips me forward, forcing me to lie face down in the dirt. "Lift that perfect ass up, Mak."

Bracing his hands by my head, Carson mounts me in a new position. He's a lot deeper in this angle. I can barely stand it. There's a fine line between pain and pleasure and Carson's dancing on it. I'll use my safe word if I have to, but going off the way my pussy feels, I don't think it's necessary. I'm slick enough to feel it all over my thighs. And whatever he's hitting inside me has my stomach clenching and feet flexing.

"Such a good girl taking this Beast's cock." His body heat warms my back. Reaching around, Carson rubs my clit while he fucks me. "You're so fucking wet."

Don't I know it. "All I keep… thinking about… is how bad I… want you… to fuck me." It's hard to talk with how hard his thrusts are.

Carson bites the back of my shoulder, and an orgasm tears through me.

It's not mine, it's his.

His cock jerks inside me and it's so hot and intense, I cry out while he roars. My heart pounds in my ears. Little dots dance in my vision. I'm still trying to catch my breath when Carson eases out of me and gently rolls me over. "You okay?"

"Yes." I love that he swipes the hair from my face so he can see me better. "That was amazing."

"We're not done yet." He kisses my forehead, then my nose, then my throat and works his way down my sweaty body until he's back with his mouth on my pussy. "I want your cum on my tongue, little vixen."

The fact that he'll have his cum on his tongue too drives me wild.

Carson nudges my thighs open and eats my pussy until I'm crying out his name with the orgasm he gives me. My clit's so sensitive it almost hurts, and I try to squirm away, but his arms are hooked around my legs and he clamps down on them to keep me immobile.

"Not yet." He growls before lapping up every drop of my climax.

And his.

When he crawls on top of me, I open my mouth, hoping like hell he understands what I want him to do next.

Carson doesn't disappoint.

He lets the cum gathered on his tongue drip onto mine. It's sweet, tart, and salty all at once.

Cum play is on both our lists, but spit play was one of the things on his. This is the first time I've tried it and I'm happy to report I'll be doing it again. It's hotter than I thought it would be.

Dragging him down to my mouth, we kiss again. It's softer and not nearly as aggressive as earlier. We taste amazing together.

We fuck amazing together too.

When Carson lifts off me again, he plucks some debris from my hair. "You sure you're okay?"

"Yeah. You?"

"Mmm." Without another word, he picks up me and carries me back to the house.

"You don't have to carry me. I can walk."

"It's not for you as much as it is for me."

I shut my mouth. Clearly part of Carson's thing is taking care of his sub, regardless of how gentle or rough a scene is. I know sometimes Doms need aftercare too.

He glances down at me, his brow furrowed. "I was really rough that time."

"Says the man with claw marks on his neck." I feel bad for scratching him that hard. Control got away from me for a moment out there. "I'm so sorry I hurt you."

"You didn't hurt me." He opens the sliding glass door, which must have been unlocked this whole time. "I'm perfectly fine."

If that's the case, why is he shaking and looking so severe?

He sets me down on the sofa and starts looking over my body. "Are you sure you're not hurt?"

"I'm fine. I swear." Me laughing only makes his body language worse. "Okay, stop, Carson. What gives?"

He runs his hands through his hair and blows out a long breath. "I just..." His jaw clenches when he looks away from me. "Fuck."

Because I'm feeling uncomfortable, I lean into humor. "Again, so soon? I thought quick recovery time was only reserved for fictional characters."

Carson's gaze swerves to mine. His mouth turns down. "What?"

"I'll fuck you again right here, right now if you want." I'm at a loss on how to make him understand that I'm totally okay. But I see that he's *not* totally okay, and I have no clue how else to make him better without reassurance.

I'll fuck the reassurance into him if I can. I'm totally down for it. I happen to have fantastic main character energy.

Carson drops to his knees and grabs my hands. His expression makes my heart droop. "You have red marks on your wrists from how hard I held you down, Mak."

"So what? We wrestled. I had to twist my arms to get out of your grip."

"I held you harder than I meant to."

"Well, I didn't notice. And I still broke free." Oh my God. What is his issue? "Carson, I loved every single thing we just did. I've never felt so free in my life. All the stress I've built up this week is gone from my chest. I feel incredible. This is exactly what I've been fantasizing about for a really, really, really long time."

He keeps staring at my wrists. Why is a

little redness bothering him? We both have bite marks and scratches on each other, but he's focused on this one small thing instead.

"Hey." I cup his face and make him look me in the eyes. "I could have used my safe word at any point, and you would have let go."

"Yeah. I would have."

"I told you before, I like it rough. I *want* marks on me, Carson."

His jaw clenches.

"Please stop beating yourself up over a couple red marks. Seriously, I'm fine."

He pulls out of my hold and sits down on the sofa next to me and buries his head in his hands. "I feel like I was too rough with you."

"You weren't. Hey…" I pull his hands down and make him look at me. "You gave me the best sex of my life just now. I want to do it again. Soon. If you get too rough, I'll say Cupcake and it'll be done. But you have to promise me the same thing, because you look like you got into a fight with a cougar, and she won."

That earns me a small laugh.

Carson pulls me onto his lap and softly says, "She did, but I somehow still got the reward."

Chapter 17

Carson

Sometimes a scene will rock a Dom, especially if it's intense, and sometimes we need reassurance that we aren't really feral beasts who've done something wrong. When Mak tries to climb out of my lap to get me some water, my arms tighten around her. "I just need to hold you for a little longer. If that's okay."

She settles against my chest and sighs. "Good. Because I really like you holding me."

Once again, I'm reminded how tiny she is. I want to put her in my pocket and keep her like a gemstone. But I can't keep her. She's not a gemstone, she's a fish. Something I can catch, admire, and will one day release back into the big ocean.

But not tonight. Tonight, she's all mine.

I'm relieved Mak isn't upset about her red wrists, but that doesn't mean I'm not angry at myself for making them like that. Rope burns, cuffs marks, chains—those things all leave marks on your body. Same for bites and scratches. And she did make it clear to me that she likes it rough…

But there's something about my hands making those same marks that hits a deep spot in my conscience and it's hard to shake it off. I've never intentionally hurt someone before. I know all too well what it's like to be on the receiving end of it and have always been very conscious of my strength and intensity.

Tonight, I let that slip.

I keep breaking my rules with Mak. I don't like it. It makes me angry with myself. I'm the one who always sets the scene. Me.

Only. Me.

But tonight, I was taken by surprise and went all in with Mak running the scene and I let myself go.

I've never done that before. Fuck… I don't know how to feel about it.

She leans against my chest and pulls a blanket over our bodies. I breathe in her scent and let it flow through my system, much like I do the lavender diffusers I keep in my studio.

Calm. Calm. Calm.

We stay cocooned for a while in silence. I can't turn my damn head off. Certain thoughts lash my conscience and I can't get them to stop. "I'm too hot." Yanking off the blanket, I still can't cool down. I'm still naked. Dirt is smeared all over me. Mak's got twigs and leaves still stuck in her hair. Plucking a stem out, I drop it to the floor. "We should clean up."

"Yeah." She doesn't sound convinced. "But I'm so comfy."

Mak wiggles her ass in my lap playfully.

This entire night feels good and strange and unplanned.

I still can't breathe. "Hop up." I gently tap her thigh and she does as I ask. My heart's beating a mile a minute. What the hell's the matter with me? Looking down at my body, sweat breaks out across my brow and down my back. My chest tightens.

"Are you okay?" Mak's brows dig into a V.

"Yeah. I'm cool." Heading to the sliding glass door, I lamely add, "I'm going to grab our clothes. Be right back."

The sooner I can calm down, the better. Yanking the door open, cool air slaps my body from all angles and I take my time gathering all our clothes from the yard and woods. Jesus Christ, we ran all over the place back here. I've honestly never had someone initiate a chase before. My submissives have always waited for me to set the scene and go over the rules ahead of time.

Mak just came out of nowhere.

I fucking loved it. But now I'm paying for the consequences of my actions. If I don't get a grasp of our dynamic and lay down better ground rules, one of us is going to have a problem. That one of us will be me.

Fuuuuuuck. What am I doing? This behavior

is so out of line for me. "Pull your shit together, dickhead. She's learning the rules. It's not her fault that you're in over your head like this."

Maybe I should go back to therapy.

Plucking her panties off the ground, I don't dare hold them to my nose again, no matter how badly I want to. Smelling her makes me an animal. I'm not ready to get hard and fuck her again so soon. My heart's still racing, and my head is all messed up.

After finding everything, I get my boxers back on and head back inside to find Mak's no longer where I left her on the couch.

Wrapped in the blanket, she's standing in front of my bookshelf again, holding a binder open. I know she heard me come in but doesn't acknowledge me until I step up behind her.

"That's an old portfolio," I say, still holding her hoodie and panties. I have no clue where her pants and shoes are.

"You took all these?" She flips through the pages like they're some kind of ancient, precious artifact she doesn't want to mess up.

"Yeah." I smile at the picture of a boy in a tuxedo, riding a bike. "That's a friend of mine's nephew."

"He's a cutie pie."

Yeah, cute, but dangerous. Beetle is a daredevil. I love that kid.

Mak flips back a few pages. "Wow. She's gorgeous."

My heart clenches. "That's my ex." The words tumble out before I have the sense to stop them. "She was a sub of mine, I mean." She's also my biggest regret.

"Her boobs are amazing." Mak stares at the picture of Lauren wearing a black leather outfit holding a cat o' nine tails in her hands. I'd taken a series of photos for the BDSM community and kept this particular one as a sample of my talent. Lauren peers down at the camera—her audience—with a powerful stance and warm eyes. She looks like she could kill you and kiss you at the same time.

"How come it didn't work out?"

Mak shared some of her hangups about her ex with me. It's only fair I reciprocate, no matter how much I hate to do it. If I never speak of Lauren again, it'll be too soon. I should have burned that damn picture long ago, instead of keeping it as a reminder of why it's important to keep my heart in a cage. "She wanted more than I could give her."

"Oh." I expect her to ask more questions, but Mak only flips the page. "This is *stunning*."

"That's in Costa Rica." The landscape shot is another favorite of mine. "The sun was setting just over the hilltop, and it made everything bleed in colors I've never seen since."

Something buzzes from the couch, where our clothing is. Recognition of the hour and who's likely calling dawns on me. "Shit." I rush over and grab my cell. "Hey. Sorry. I'm not going to make it tonight."

Mak turns to me and closes the binder.

"Okay, no problem," Trey says. "If you change your mind, you know where to find us."

"Yeah." I hang up and guilt claws its way up my chest when I look at Mak. "Sorry about that."

"No, no." She slides the binder back on the shelf. "I'm the one who's sorry. I didn't realize you had plans, and I took over your night. I'll leave."

I step in her way, blocking her from the clothing on the couch. "I don't want you to go." Which is exactly why I should usher her right out my front door this minute. "I didn't have plans. That was just some friends of mine seeing if I was going online tonight."

She studies me for a moment and licks her lips. "Well, please don't let me stop you, Carson." Her tone is gentle and sweet. She's not acting dejected, which makes this easier. Mak slips past me to grab her things. "I'll call you later this week?"

"Stay." My voice cracks, just like my heart. "Please… stay."

We stare at each other for a long minute.

"Stay with me." For fuck's sake, I sound like a child. "We can watch a movie or order takeout if you want."

"I'll stay on one condition." She drops her

blanket and slips back on my hoodie. "I'll stay if you go online with your friends and do whatever it is you had originally planned for tonight."

Hell to the no. "It's just video games." And there's no way I'm playing them when Mak's over. I'd rather give her all my attention. "It's not important."

"It was important enough for them to call you and check in."

I want to argue. I want to downplay it. I want to do a lot of things and can't because this will only work with Mak if I'm open and honest with her. "It's how I decompress."

And after what just happened, and the way my head's all mixed up, I really need an outlet.

She nods as if that makes sense.

"Do you play?" If she did, she'd be the most perfect creature on the planet.

"No, I never really got into video games."

She's still the most perfect creature on the planet.

"How about you play, and I'll..." Mak saunters over to my bookshelf again and plucks a paperback off the top shelf. "Read."

A smile streaks across my face. "Deal."

Chapter 18

Mak

"Is this where you keep the dead bodies?" I follow him into his basement, holding onto the railing with one hand, clutching a shifter romance with a half-naked hottie on the cover with the other.

"Nah, I keep those in a spare bedroom upstairs. They're set up like dolls at a tea party."

"Sweet." My feet hit the bottom of the steps just as he turns on the lights. "Whoa."

Carson's basement is set up like a giant gaming station. I'm talking neon lights, huge couch, speakers all around, and blacklights that make the swirly carpet glow in purples and blues. There's a massive flat screen TV across from the leather couch and a desk with huge monitors and keyboards on it against the far wall with a black and green chair that looks like it should be a prop in a sci-fi movie.

"Decompressing requires a lot of…" I look around again. "Stimulation."

When Carson smiles, his teeth glow thanks to all the blacklights.

This man is an enigma. His studio was one thing, but his house is like three levels of the twilight zone. On the top floor, he has the BDSM bedroom made of dark fantasies. His main level is all comfort and functional living. And his bottom level is some next level video game/arcade heaven.

There's even a bar and fridge.

I'm starting to think Carson has a lot of facets to him, all of which I'm thoroughly enjoying so far.

"You sure about this?" He rubs the back of his neck and is still only wearing his boxer briefs. I swear I can't figure out how we got this comfortable with each other. I like it, but I'm also freaking out about it. "We can just watch a movie. Or go out to dinner? We can do anything you want, Mak."

"I know. And I want this." I shake my book at him. "I just worked a double, Carson, then got fucked hard in the woods afterwards. I could use a little decompression myself." I'm only half lying. The real truth is, I'm growing attached to this man and I like how comfortable he makes me feel. I want to be with him doing normal stuff too, not just kinky things.

I don't think I realized how lonely I've been until Carson came into my life. Sure, I've had a couple hookups since my big breakup, but this feels way different. He's not a rebound by any means, and yet I can't put a label on what this really is. Partnership doesn't cut it. Situationship doesn't either.

I'm getting attached too soon.

But I tried to leave, didn't I? He had plans, and I crashed them and offered to hit the road. *He's* the one who asked me to stay. And how could I possibly refuse seeing one more side of this perfect man?

"If you get bored, or if I'm too loud, just… throw something at my head."

"Okay." I won't.

"And really…" Carson hits some buttons on his computer. "I can quit at any point. Just let me know and I'll stop playing."

Dropping onto the couch, ready to curl up with a good book, I hope he plays all night long. "I'm about to get acquainted with a hot billionaire werewolf who owns a sex club. Stop trying to interrupt this magical meet cute."

All three of Carson's computer screens light up and sound blasts through the speakers, making my heart leap out of my chest.

"Shit, sorry!" He rushes to turn down the volume. "I like a fully submerged experience." He chuckles as if embarrassed. "I'll wear my headphones so I don't disturb you and your billionaire werewolf alpha Dom."

"No, no, no. I want to hear your game, too."

He frowns. "Won't that distract you from reading?"

"Nope. I like noise when I read." No clue why. "I usually blast music at home when I'm enjoying my smut."

Carson cranks the volume up only a little, but with the surround sound, it's enough to rumble my chest.

"Heyyyyy!" A woman yells. "Dickhead's back!"

Carson grabs a small mic on his desk. "I knew you'd miss me, Ara."

Someone else gets on the line and his voice is mega deep. "Damn, it's been a while. Trey said you weren't playing tonight. Glad you changed your mind."

"Yeah, sorry. I was distracted." Carson swirls his chair and winks at me. "I'm ready to hand Trey his balls. He won't have to beg me again."

"I've never begged a day in my life."

"Well, that's a damn lie." Ara says. "You beg Erin for — eeeep! Glitch!"

"Do *not* finish that sentence, Kitty."

I drop my book to cover my mouth because I'm laughing so hard. His friends sound fun.

"Please leave all honorifics at the door. I don't want my innocent ears to bleed." Carson flicks his fingers across some keys and the screens change. "And by the way, I have company. Mak, say hi."

"Hi!" I sound ridiculously chipper, even to my own ears.

Silence echoes in the room. Then suddenly Trey says, "Mak? Clap once if you're being held hostage."

"I'm gonna clap you in a motherfucking minute," Carson growls. "Knock it off, asshole. She's trying to read smut and you're ruining her vibe."

"Ohhh. What book is it?" Ara asks.

Carson rattles off the title before I even look at it.

"I haven't read that one yet," Ara pouts.

"It's good. He's got two dicks, I think." Trey's voice is muffled for a minute. "Shit, I thought Beetle was within earshot. He's not. Christ, that was close. Anyways, that's a good one. The cover was the fastest I've ever made to date, too. The author is easy to please."

"Yeah," Carson laughs. "Chloe went out with the model the night I took those cover shots. He did not, in fact, have two dicks. According to her, he barely even had one."

"Bummer." Ara laughs. "We can't all have a unicorn demon."

"I'm not even going to ask what that means," Carson says.

"Speaking of covers…" Trey speaks louder. "I let my client know you were on it. She's thrilled and wanted me to reiterate she's really into Florence and the Machine vibes. What the fuck is that anyway?"

"An indie rock band. Broaden your musical

horizons, man." Carson leans back and swivels impatiently in his chair. "Are we chit chatting all night or getting this game started, fuckers?"

This is not a side of Carson I've seen yet. He's mouthy as hell. I can't imagine being trash-talked by my friends like these guys are going at it with each other. But the more zingers they toss each other, the more I like it.

"I'm gonna fuck your mom and give her a son she actually loves," Trey says to Carson at one point.

Ara cracks up laughing.

I think someone gets points or dies or I don't even know what, but Carson stands up and shouts. A figure on the screen glitches and respawns.

"Distract him for us, Mak!" Ara yells. "Put the book down and help us!"

"She can't help you, Ara. She's banging a werewolf billionaire at an underground sex club." Carson's furiously slamming his fingers on the keyboard. "Suck it, fools!"

I've yet to start my book because I'm enjoying this crazy entertainment. With Carson's back still to me, I pull off my—*his*—hoodie, and saunter over to where he's furiously hitting the keys to win the game.

I rest my bare hip against his desk.

"Oh shit." His gaze slowly scales down my body. "Ohhh shhhhiit."

"Can they see me?" I mouth.

He swallows hard, his eyes wide as he shakes his head.

Good.

"Get him, Mak!" Ara yells.

"Quit bugging her. And stop trying to cheat your way to a win." Carson watches with a predatory gaze as I sink down to my knees under his desk. His breathing speeds up when I hook my fingers into the waistband of his boxers and pull them down his thick thighs.

His hard dick bobs as it springs free, and I capture it with my mouth.

"I respawned someplace else. Shit!" Trey yells. "Damnit, hang on. I'm back in the T-zone."

"Your brother did a great job on this game." Ara's voice is light and bubbly. "Nice graphics."

Trey makes some noise in the background. "Carson, you still with us?"

"Yeah." He clears his throat. "I'm… in the R zone. How the fuck did I get heeeeerrrrrrrre *fuuuuck.*" Carson clutches the top of my head as I suck him off.

His gaze is locked on me, not the game.

I pull away and pump him with my hands. "Play your game and let me play mine."

Opening my mouth wide—because Carson's girthy—I go down on him again. I can't get him past a certain point in my throat at this angle, but I've got a good bit of him between my lips and start sucking in earnest while he tries to focus on the game.

The sounds of everyone yelling, guns blazing, avatars running and fighting music all fade away.

Carson growls like an animal, fisting my hair and pumping his hips in slow thrusts.

It's suddenly very quiet and all I can hear are the sounds he's making and the slurping noises from me.

"That's it, Mak. Suck my cock with that hot, pretty mouth."

I scrape his thighs, which earns me another growl from him. Fuck a billionaire werewolf, I've got my own fantasy man right where I want him—about to come down my throat.

"Shhhhiiittt you feel so fucking good." Carson's breaths turn ragged the longer I blow him. "Swallow me."

His cock swells and legs stiffen a few seconds before he orgasms. My tongue's flat against his shaft and I love how his dick throbs between my lips as he shoots salty, sweet cum into my mouth. I'm not wasting a drop of this goodness. Sucking him until he begs me to let go and show mercy, I swipe my hand over my chin to clean off my drool.

I like giving messy blowjobs. And I love the way Carson's looking down at me right now.

"Did you win?" I whisper so his friends can't hear me.

"Yeah," he pants. "I fucking did." Carson

grips my arms and helps me crawl out from under his desk.

"What's your score?" Wait. All the monitors have been turned off. "I thought you—"

Carson smashes his mouth to mine and lifts me off the ground. "That was naughty of you."

"You mean that was very giving of me." I yelp when he drops me on the couch. "What are you doing? You're supposed to be playing your game!"

"I'd rather play yours, little vixen." He snatches the book I'd discarded and hands it to me. "Start reading."

Confusion makes me silent. But then he drops down by my feet and spreads my legs. "Start. Reading. Out loud."

While I try to mutter out the first sentence, Carson descends on my pussy and puts his trash-talking mouth to good use. That double-dicked billionaire werewolf is nothing compared to my man.

With Carson's devious tongue fucking me, I don't even get through the first page.

Chapter 19

Carson

It's been a week since Mak left my house. I still can't stop thinking about her. We've texted a bit, but she hasn't come over again, and I've yet to visit her place. The tension growing in my chest hurts like a bitch. I can't get her out of my mind.

It's unsettling.

I'm not a fan of attachments. I'm not into instalove or even instalust. I need a lot of things working together in just the right way for it to speak a language I'll respond to. That probably sounds high maintenance, but I've never claimed to be perfect. I'm nowhere close to it.

Mak didn't spend the night after I made her come three times on my tongue while she tried to groan, grind, and grunt through one page of that smut book. I wanted her to stay, but she declined. I had to bite my tongue to stop myself from begging her. Mak was being smarter than I was by leaving when she did.

Only now I can't concentrate on shit.

I've got a convention coming up, two art

shows to attend, and I'm still waiting to hear back about a contest I submitted to. Not to mention thousands of boudoir photos to sift through and edit. Plus, I have a book signing to plan for where I'll be taking photos of authors doing their thing and now I need to make sure I can schedule time with some of the cover models joining them. Every opportunity that comes my way, I take when it's career driven.

I also have three back-to-back sessions today at the studio.

My life is busy enough without adding pining over a woman to my to do list.

Speaking of photos, I never did show Mak hers. I keep thinking I can use it as a tactic to bring her back to my house again, but why bother? I don't need an excuse. I can ask her to come over and she either will or she won't. The files will be emailed to her regardless. I just haven't done it yet.

Why am I floundering?

Damnit, this woman is fucking me up.

"Hey boss, you want a coffee?"

I look up at Chloe and sigh. "Yeah. Get me whatever is strongest. I don't even care if it tastes good or not." I'm dog tired because I haven't slept in days and no amount of jerking off, lifting weights, or tv will ease my anxiety. Might as well feed the demon some caffeine to make it worse.

I've got about an hour before my next

client comes in. I should be setting up for it. Instead, I pull out my cell and scroll through my contacts to find the one I haven't called since my last downward spiral.

They pick up on the second ring. "Hey, man. It's been a long fucking time."

"Yeah. Sorry. It's been crazy busy. How are things going for you?"

"Good as it gets." There's silence for a moment. "What's up? You and I both know you didn't call without a good reason."

My ass drops onto the bed I should be remaking. "I think I fucked up."

"Go on."

"I got a new sub last week. She's…" *Amazing, sweet, spectacular.* "Fun."

"Fun is good." Caution laces my old mentor's voice. "Fun is important."

My confession flies out of me. "I've-broken-nearly-every-rule-I-have." Standing up, I pace like a caged jaguar in my studio. "She was new on K!nkLink. I didn't even think to research her first before sending her contract. Then we just *clicked.* I can't even describe it."

"I fail to see the problem."

"I've broken every rule in the book. And I do mean every fucking rule, Ryker."

Silence stretches through our cellphones. It makes me feel guilty. I want to punch something.

My own nuts would be a perfect target.

"Did you hurt her?" Ryker's tone is edgy and dark with aggression.

I stop short. "What? No, asshole, of course not!"

"Then you didn't break *every* rule in the book."

"I gripped her wrists." Thinking about it now makes me feel sick. "They were red afterwards."

"As wrists often get when something's around them. How did she react to it?"

"She said it was fine."

"Do you believe her?"

"Yes." Mak would have said something if she wasn't okay with it. "She's vocal and sincere. And she likes it rough. She said it didn't bother her at all, but it bothers the fuck out of me." I never dreamed I'd get this way about something so trivial, but here we are.

Ryker clears his throat. "Aside from her wrists, what else is eating at you, Carson?"

Too many things. "I didn't go slow. She's new and I moved like she's not."

"And what happened?"

"She dropped hard and fast the first time. I didn't even know her comforts for aftercare. I had to wing it." Something that I'll never forgive myself for, honestly.

"And the second time? I assume there's been more than one."

"She initiated it."

Silence over the line again.

"And?" Ryker finally asks.

"I lost my self-control." Admitting that out loud makes me want to jump out the fucking window. "That's when I hurt her wrists."

"Hurt is not the same as redden. You know this."

I don't need Ryker splitting hairs on the subject. "I don't like that I did that to her."

"Then work harder on your control. Being protective is very much a part of your nature, Carson. I still don't…" He pauses and I hold my breath. There's a reason I called Ryker and not Trey or Glitch or anyone else I'm close to. "Describe her to me."

There it is. He knows why I'm downward spiraling. "Five foot tall, about a hundred-twenty pounds."

"Mmm hmm."

My body grows hot and my stomach rolls as shame hits me.

"She's your first spinner, isn't she?"

A growl rumbles out of my throat. "Don't call her that."

It's not that I have an issue with the term, but I don't like the idea of Ryker imagining what my girl would look like on my dick. I don't want him imagining her at all.

Damnit, why am I turning into such a possessive beast about her?

"I think we both know it's not that you

reddened her wrists, that has you this rocked. It's the size of her wrists. The size of *her* compared to *you*."

I shouldn't have come to him. Being called out is not what I need right now.

"Putting your body image issues aside for a moment," Ryker says with a stricter, colder tone. "If she initiated it the second time, after you floundered her aftercare, then take that as a win. She gave you a second chance."

"And I fucked it up by going too hard!"

"Or did you give her exactly what she wanted? She has a safe word, correct?" He doesn't wait for me to answer. "Did she use it when you held her wrists?"

"No."

"No." Like that's that. End of story. Case closed.

Running a hand down my face, I squeeze my eyes shut. "I'm growing attached." There. I said it. "It's stupid, I know. And it's too fast. But I think I'm feeling… feelings."

"Think or know?"

"I—"

"Don't let what happened between you and Lauren fuck this up, Carson. You wasted a lot of time over that woman. She doesn't get to impact your present or your future."

"My biggest rule is to not get attached."

"Some rules are meant to get broken." Ryker huffs in my ear. "Christ, man, you can't keep yourself frozen forever. If your sub is—"

"Mak. Her name is Mak." I can't handle him thinking she's just a submissive when I'm now realizing she might be more than that to me.

"Mak. I like it."

I wish I hadn't told him now. He says her name in too nice of a way. I don't even want her name in his mouth.

Holy hell, I'm a clusterfuck.

"Look," Ryker says. "Mak's giving you what you need, and you're giving her what she needs, and that's exactly what this life is for. If you find yourself getting comfortable, even out of scenes with her, that's not a bad thing. You're still working on yourself, right?"

"Always."

"Can she touch you without a problem?"

I hate that he even had to ask. "Yes. And she can't seem to keep her hands off me. As long as I don't look, I'm good with it."

"That's a step in the right direction, Carson."

I know. "But this feels like too much, too soon. We're nowhere near a point where I should be feeling like this. I can't eat. I can't sleep. I fucking miss her when she's not with me."

Ryker sighs like this is worse than he thought. Or maybe he's thinking I'm being a tool and doesn't know how to hang up with me.

"How do your expectations for the future line up?"

"I have no clue, other than we both don't want to be married or have kids."

"You're worried this is a repeat of Lauren, aren't you?"

Fuck right I am. "I don't think I can go through an ugly breakup like that again, Ryker."

Squeezing my eyes shut, I can still see Lauren crying, her mascara running in black streaks down her cheeks as she takes kitchen shears and cuts off the collar I'd commissioned to symbolize our commitment.

I wore the key around my neck, and she had the lock on hers. I was crazy in love with that woman. Blinded by it enough to never see the red flags or that she was unhappy with me. I believed I finally had a win in my lonely life and spent every waking moment making sure she was happy and cared for. I lost who I was so that I could be the man she needed.

But Lauren wanted more than I could give her. In the beginning, when I was up front about what I wanted and didn't want in my life, she'd said she felt the same way as me.

But the bliss didn't last.

Eventually, Lauren wanted commitments I didn't want to make, and babies I couldn't give her. She screamed at me for being selfish and said if I loved her like I said I did, that I'd get a reverse vasectomy for her. I tossed back that I didn't want kids and couldn't understand why she'd changed her mind so suddenly.

She said she'd lied to me since the beginning. Lauren admitted that she assumed if we were together long enough, I'd eventually change my mind and give her everything she was missing in her life.

Her confession was a battering ram to my gut, my pride, and my heart smashed to a pulp because of it. When I dropped to my knees and begged her to stay with me, she threw the destroyed collar in my face and looked me dead ass in the eyes and said, *"You're not enough for me."*

The possibility of Mak doing the same to me makes my blood turn icy. I refuse to put myself back in the line of fire like that, which is why I have the no falling in love rule in the first place.

But who am I kidding? This isn't love. "It's probably just infatuation." I attempt to laugh it off like this is no big deal. "I'm being a dramatic idiot."

Ryker doesn't respond, which makes me believe he agrees.

"I'm sorry I called you with this, man. I didn't mean to waste your time."

"You never waste my time, Carson. But…" There's more shuffling and I hear cars honking in the background. "I stand by what I said earlier. Some rules are made to be broken. Let yourself have the possibility that this time can be different. You're bound to meet your match at some point. Maybe this woman is it."

I'm scared he's right.

I'm scared he's wrong.

"I wasn't looking for more than a play partner."

Ryker chuckles. "Yeah, well, sometimes we find more than we're looking for. Good luck."

He hangs up on me.

Chapter 20

Mak

Other than some playful texts, I haven't really talked to Carson in over two weeks. It sucks, but my shifts at work have been all over the place since three of our staff left. I was assured replacements are coming, which I'm grateful for, but until then, I've been working myself into the ground.

It makes me crave Carson in a way I wasn't expecting. He gives me something I haven't had before, and I don't even know if there's a name for it.

He's like a hike—beautiful, hard, challenging, exhilarating, and relaxing all at once. My body aches after we're done fucking, but my mind is peacefully blissed out and not even an atomic bomb could wipe the smile from my face afterwards.

Good God, I've really been dickmatized.

Except it's not just his cock, and tongue, and hands… it's the way he cares for me before, during, and afterwards. It's the way he holds me close, and his body temp seeps into mine. The way he drizzles chocolate in my tea. How he rubs my legs when we talk on the couch. We're keeping each other at arm's length in some ways and devouring each other when we let our guards down.

That's not normal, is it?

Shit, I don't have a clue. I'm honestly really confused. I can't stop thinking about him. The moment I left his house, I missed him. That's fucking crazy. This isn't love, or perfection—it's only the "honeymoon" phase where we're still new and excited to explore each other—and we're being on our best behavior.

That night with the video games and book was such a red flag. We fucked like animals outside then came in and turned into an old couple doing our individual hobbies.

That's level 5 on the relationship scale.

Shouldn't we still be down at level 1 or 2?

"Earth to Mak." Leah snaps her fingers in my face. "You in there, babe?"

I blink and pick up my tea. "Yeah." *Sip, sip.* "Sorry, I zoned out. I'm exhausted."

"I bet. It should be criminal to have you guys working around the clock like that."

"It's fine. We get breaks." Not that I take any. "I'm just happy I finally have off for a couple days."

"Any plans?"

"Sleep, sleep, and more sleep."

Leah looks disappointed. "No Carson?"

I don't even want to think about Carson right now. It makes my belly flip flop every time I do. "What do you have going on?"

"I have a date later tonight. Tomorrow, I am going to my mom's birthday party. That's about it."

I take another sip of my London fog, wincing because it's already getting too cold to be enjoyable. "That should be fun."

Leah places her elbows on the table and tucks her fists under her chin. "My date's with Carson."

"Mmm hmm."

"We're going to a sex club."

"Sounds fun."

"I'm going to blow him in his car while he sings metalcore to me."

"Yay." I blink slowly and take another sip of my crappy tea.

"Damnit, Mak!" Leah smacks the table. "Come on. We're taking you home."

I scrub my face and yawn. "No. I'm good. I swear. What are your plans this weekend?"

"You didn't hear a single word I just said, did you?"

"Mmm hmm." Nope.

"That's it. Come on." She grabs my hand and yanks me out of my chair. I don't bother taking my tea because it really tastes awful. Leah opens the door to the café for me and I end up bumping into someone.

"Oh, sorry." My vision's blurry from fatigue.

"Mak?" It takes me a second to focus and realize it's Chloe. "Hey!" She leans in and gives me a big hug like we're old friends. It's not fake. This is really how I think she is with everyone she meets. "I'm going in for cup number seven."

"Enjoy," I say, too tired to give more than a half-smile and a flimsy wave.

Her expression shifts from bubbly to concerned. "You feel okay?"

"Yeah. I'm good. It was so good to bump into you." Because I'm awkward, I lean in and give her another hug, then Leah and I head to our cars.

"You're a mess, Mak." She opens the door for me. "I don't think you should drive home."

I start the engine, slap my cheeks a couple times, and put down all my windows to let all the cold air in. "I'll be fine. Promise. I don't have too far to go."

"Still..." Leah's not convinced. "I should drive you."

"No, I'm fine." I crank up some music and that helps. "I'll text you when I get home so you know I'm not dead."

"Good girl."

I take off and manage to make it all the way home, and to the couch, where I fall face first into the cushions.

•••

You ever fall asleep so hard that when you wake up you don't know what time it is, or what year it is, or what planet you're on? That's me now. I blink and can barely make out the blurry numbers on the clock by my TV. Grasping for my cell, I end up finding it on the floor and see I have several missed calls from Leah.

Shit. I'm in trouble.

Voice message one: Hey, where are you? You said you'd call when you got home, and you haven't.

Voice message two: Damnit, Mak. Call me back or answer my texts. Fuck it. I'm coming over.

Voice message three: You dumb bitch, you had me worried sick. Glad you're home. Yes, I did a drive by. And I could literally hear you snoring through the door to your apartment. You sound like a warthog, did you know that? Love you, babe.

The back of my head hits the sofa cushion, and I rub my eyes, sighing. I feel so much better having slept, but this is going to wreck my already precarious sleep schedule.

Mak: Sorry. I legit crashed the instant I stepped inside my house.

Leah: Tell your boss I said she's a dick for making you work yourself into that level of fatigue.

Mak: Will do. Love you.

Leah: Love you too.

Settling back on my couch, I can't tell if I want to attempt going back to sleep or if I should just get up and be productive at… what time is it?

Crap, it's two in the morning. I can't vacuum or blast loud music while I scrub my tub at this hour because it might wake the neighbors. Have I mentioned how much I hate this apartment? The walls are paper thin, and no one is friendly. I can't wait to move out in a month.

Oh! That's what I can do. Go back on my endless search for places to rent before I'm out of time and get stuck renewing my lease here.

Grabbing a blanket off the back of my couch, I get comfortable and scroll through my options. Frustration slams into me within five minutes. There's nothing I like. It makes me feel trapped and I hate it.

I wish I had a house like Carson's. Not as big, but something that's away from everyone else. I'll never be able to afford that on my own. Not in this area, at least. And I don't want to move too far away from my work because that would just make more problems that I don't have the energy to tackle.

I really need to reevaluate my life. I love my job, but it's killing me and I'm starting to resent it. For over a year, retaining staff has been a growing issue, and since I'm the single one with no life, I always get asked to take on someone else's shift—whether they're sick, it's a holiday, or they want to spend extra time with their family.

At first, I said yes, without hesitation. I get it. Lots of my colleagues are married with little kids and who would want to work on Christmas morning when you have toddlers? I didn't mind. In fact, I offered first.

Then people started taking advantage of my kindness, and it hasn't stopped.

It's a pattern for me that I realized too late. It took coming to a breaking point with He-who-was-a-waste-of-time for me to see that my compassion and generosity are easily used against me. Breaking up with him was the best thing I'd ever done for myself.

Joining K!nkLink, so far, is turning out to be the second best thing I've ever done for myself.

Maybe finding a new employer will be the third best thing.

Or I need to be patient because new hires *are* coming and then work life won't be so crazy.

Abandoning my search for a new apartment, I login into the kink app. Not sure why, other than I kind of just want to stare at Carson's profile pic.

Damn, he's hot.

My hand slips down my stomach and

between my thighs. Shimmying out of my scrubs, I play with my pussy, slowly running the pad of my finger in circles on my clit while I stare at his mouth. His perfect, full, soft, kissable lips are curved into a devious smile.

I've felt what that mouth of his can do to my cunt. My mind hooks on to the memory of his fat tongue and how fast he can flick it, how deep he can penetrate it into my pussy. I start fingering myself, wishing with all my might that I could make him magically crawl out of this picture and fuck me like he did in his backyard.

He's so sexy. So big. So observant and stern, yet gentle and patient. Carson's a wild mix of pleasures and discoveries—all built for my pleasure.

I stare at his big, brown eyes and black hair. Then I drop my gaze to his perfectly sloped nose. Finally, I latch onto his snakebites. I finger myself harder and bite my bottom lip when I feel an orgasm build. Tension mounts. Dropping my phone, I use both hands to pleasure myself, imagining Carson's body hovering over mine. *He's collaring my throat with his hand, squeezing it just enough to make me tense. His teeth graze my shoulder just before he bites down. The heat from his body warming me up...*

"That's it, little vixen. Fuck yourself for me. I want to hear it. I want to smell it. I want to taste it."

Rubbing my clit faster, harder, I plunge two fingers into my pussy. I wish he was here. I wish it was his cock inside me. His mouth on me. His hands on me. I want to hear him growl in my ear.

"Fuck me, Carson." My back bows and heels digging into the cushions as I add a third finger and try to make myself come with his image plastered on the backs of my eyelids.

The climax was hard to chase, but I finally manage to tip over the edge. Pleasure washes over me like I've slid into a refreshing pool on a hot summer's day. It lasts for a few seconds and dies out.

How... underwhelming.

Popping my eyes open, I sink into disappointment. After having wild sex with Carson, my worst fear has been solidified: Nothing else will compare to him.

I need a lot going on at once to make my brain click into pleasure mode. It's why I gravitated towards primal play. Even after my first time with Carson, when I crashed in a frenzy of mixed emotions, I'd never come so hard in my goddamn life.

Until I came even harder the second time we did a hunt and chase, when I'd surprised him in his backyard.

Picking up my cell again, I stare at his picture. "You've ruined me for any other man." Unshed tears make my dark apartment blurry.

He's shown me how precious and powerful patience and vulnerability are. He's given me adrenaline rushes not even roller coasters can come close to. He's provided me with safety and acceptance while letting me play out my fantasies in a safe way. He's soft and sweet. He's strong and savage. He's—

Online.

Panic and jealousy clog my throat.

It's quickly squashed when a chat bubble pops up.

WolfByte: Boo.

I giggle, despite the unease trying to slither into my belly. Why is he on here? Is he looking for someone else? Wouldn't that be a breach of our contract? Does he want to end things with me so soon?

Chill, Mak…

Pricurious: Boo back.

I wait for him to say something else. When he doesn't, I type something to fill the silence and erase everything before I hit send. This happens three times and then my cell rings.

Shit.

"Hey."

"Heyyy," he purrs in a deep, sleepy voice. "Didn't expect to see you online."

I think there's jealousy in his tone, or maybe I'm just reading into things too much. "I couldn't sleep."

"Me either."

"Why are you on the app?" The question blows out of me like a hurricane, but my voice is small and fragile. I hate that I'm being insecure. We signed a contract. We're exclusive to each other. He's not going to cheat on me.

Why would I care if he did? We're not a couple.

I feel queasy.

"You probably don't want to know the answer," he says, laughing. "Why are you on?"

Anger surges in my veins, but I don't dare give it a voice. "You probably don't want to know the answer."

I'm not about to tell him that I missed him so much I stared at the only picture of him I have access to and got myself off on it.

"Tell me anyway," he says in a slightly guarded tone. At least, I imagine it sounds that way.

"Honestly?"

"If we aren't truthful with each other, Mak, this will never work." His tone is clipped and definitely guarded.

He's right. I should just be open and honest. For all I know, he thinks I'm on here looking for someone new.

"I was getting myself off on your profile picture." Silence fills my ears, which makes me paranoid. "Are you there, or did I lose you?"

He growls into my ear and my heart rate speeds up. "How many times did you come?"

"Just once."

"Only once?"

"It wasn't… exciting enough to try for another." I smack my forehead and squeeze my eyes shut. I can't believe I just said that.

"You going to be up for a while?"

"Yeah, I suppose." I glance at the clock again. "I crashed after work and now my sleep schedule is all messed up. Not that it wasn't already screwy from the shifts I've been working, but I woke up and couldn't even tell what year it is. Annnnd now I guess I have my second wind because I can't seem to shut up."

I hear the rumble of an engine on the other end of the line.

"What's your address?"

I sit up. "Huh?"

"Text me your address, Mak. I'm on my way to your house. If I have to knock on every goddamn door in the county to find you, I will. But the sooner to you tell me where to go, the sooner I can make you come properly."

Excitement rushes through me like white water rapids. I spout out my address and I swear my cheeks tingle with adrenaline.

"I'm on my way. See you in twenty."

Chapter 21

Carson

When I saw that little light pop up on Mak's profile in that stupid fucking app, I nearly lost my shit. My insecurities include, but are not limited to, feeling inadequate. Surprise, surprise. And the first thing I thought of when I saw her online was that she wasn't happy with our arrangement and was searching for another Dom.

Big assumption, I know, but I've had experiences with submissives being unfaithful and breaching our contracts—except for the one that was so loyal she ripped my heart out with a steak knife, chewed it up, and spat it back in my face. *Thanks, Lauren.*

After dissecting everything Ryker said to me, I was finally able to reel myself back in and finished my workday on a higher note. But the fact that I haven't heard from her in two weeks hasn't sat well with me. I wanted to give her space. I'm sure she's as busy as I am and we're not a priority to each other yet.

At least I'm not to her. Which is completely

fine. I haven't reached out to her either, so the problem goes both ways.

But when Chloe mentioned she saw Mak in the café earlier today and said she seemed "off", I'd be a liar to say I didn't panic a little.

I'm in trouble. I've grown attached to a woman who I have no business feeling feelings for. It makes me want to simultaneously bust a U-turn and leave town, and also break every traffic law to reach her faster just so I can hold her in my arms.

Mak's giving me a headfuck and a half without even trying.

So I went online tonight with the intention of going over her profile to see if I could conjure a scene for us that didn't hit any of her limits. I had her likes and dislikes memorized, but I've questioned my unraveling mind too much lately and wanted to double check.

Now here I am, with my plans thwarted, because I'm too eager to make my girl come.

I pull into her apartment complex and slam my door shut harder than I mean to. The whole building is dark except for two windows on the second floor. I hit the button with *M Johnson* written on it and she buzzes me in.

My heart pounds as I skip steps to reach her floor faster. She swings open the door before I have a chance to knock. Her hair's wet as if she just got out of the shower. Dressed in little booty shorts and an oversized t-shirt with the neckline all stretched out, Mak looks like the perfect midnight snack.

My dick hardens instantly.

"Hi," she says, waving.

I respond by slamming my mouth to hers, driving her backwards, and kicking her door closed with my foot. *Slam!* I don't care if I wake the neighbors or not. All I want is to devour this woman. Let their jaws drop and pulses race when she screams through her orgasms for everyone in a ten-mile radius to hear.

Mak climbs me like a tree, and I cup her ass with one hand, while clutching the nape of her neck with the other and deepen our kiss. Holy shit, she's just as ravenous as I am. Her tongue twirls around mine, fighting for dominance.

Slamming her against the wall, I hook her legs under my arms and lift her until her pussy is in my face. Mak's hands smack the ceiling as she holds her balance. "Oh my God, Carson."

I bite her pussy through the flimsy shorts she's got on. Keeping her pressed to the wall, I brace Mak's torso with one hand and shove her shorts to the side so I can have access to what I crave. She smells like Heaven. Tastes like it too once I get my first lick.

Two weeks of not seeing this woman and I'm a wild beast.

My body has never been so desperate, nor has my soul been this deprived before.

I tongue fuck my girl until her thighs

clamp around my head and her body shakes. Mak's quick orgasm floods my tastebuds and I shove my tongue as deep as I can to feel her convulsions. It's exquisite. Once I've savored every last drop, I lower her down on wobbly legs. "Where's your bedroom?"

She points in the direction of where I want her next and I waste zero time scooping her into my arms to take her there. Her house is a mess. Books and clothes are all over the floor. Her bed looks like an explosion of blankets. It smells like fresh laundry and roses.

Laying her down, I kiss her neck, loving how she's pulling on my shirt.

"I want to rip this thing off you." She growls like a feral kitten and tears at it with no success.

She's so goddamn adorable.

"Here." I get it started for her and rip the neckline. "Now try."

Her eyes light up with determination. With her cheeks bright pink and lips swollen from our kisses, Mak grips my t-shirt again and tears it clean down the middle. *Rrrrrrip*! "Oh!" She gasps triumphantly. "Holy moly, that was so satisfying." She slips it off my arms, and it falls to the floor.

While I loom over her, forcing her to lie back on the bed, she keeps running her greedy hands all over my arms and chest. "You're so sexy, Carson."

I'm glad she thinks so.

Before Mak reaches lower, I growl and catch her bottom lip between my teeth to suck it into my mouth. Positioned between her legs, I lift her hands up and pin them above her head. Mak wraps her legs around my waist, her heels shoving into my lower back as if she's trying to draw me in closer to her.

I kiss down her neck, inhaling the sweet scent of her shampoo. Letting go of her hands, I'm halfway down her body, trailing kisses all over her soft skin when, she suddenly squirms away, too fast for me to stop.

A devious smile spreads across her face.

My gaze narrows. "What are you up to, Mak?"

"You want me so bad? Come get me, Big Boy." She scampers backwards with a wicked gleam in her eyes. Suddenly, her hand slips off the edge of the bed and she falls onto the floor. "Whoop!"

"Oh shit!" My heart clatters in my throat as I crawl across the bed and look over the edge. "Are you okay?"

Her head tips back and she bursts out laughing. "So much for being sexy."

I'm falling for this woman so hard, I fear I'll shatter to a million pieces when I hit the ground. "I don't know, you look pretty sexy to me."

She's still cackle-laughing as she climbs

back on the bed. "Glad you think so."

Mak straddles my hips and kisses me again. It's soft and attentive and makes my goddamn toes curl. While I run my hands up and down her body, she fumbles with the buckle to my jeans. My chest expands and contracts with my heavy breathing. It's hard to keep myself in check when I want to dominate every aspect of this moment.

Her small, chilled hands on my skin remind me that I have to be careful. I can't be too rough with Mak, or I might hurt her.

My cock springs free from my pants and she growls like a baby tiger while pulling them down my thighs. She glances up at me through her curtain of thick, wet hair. Crawling over my body again, I'm vaguely aware that she's still completely dressed, and I've somehow become naked.

Vulnerability darkens my mind.

"I want your cock in my mouth, Carson."

She sucks me off until those dark insecurities of mine are chased away by pleasure. It's not long before I'm clutching her hair, fucking her mouth at a pace I enjoy, relishing the slurping sounds she makes while deep throating me. "That's a good girl. Use that pretty mouth on me."

Mak's lashes flutter, her eyes watering as she stares up at me a second before my balls tighten and I unload in her mouth. My body is so tight I could snap. Once the last of my climax shudders through me, my girl spits all my cum back onto my dick.

I growl in appreciation. "Damn, that's hot."

She doesn't say a word when she slips out of her clothing and mounts me. Grabbing her hips, I stare at her with hooded eyes, wondering if I can take much more of her touch.

"Can you keep going?" Mak asks, running her pussy along my now semi-hard shaft.

I kiss her as my response and within seconds, I'm hard as steel again. I doubt I'll be able to come a second time, but that doesn't mean I can't fuck her into oblivion. She lowers herself down on my dick slowly, using my cum and her arousal as lubrication.

"Open," she demands, holding my throat.

It takes me a hot second to obey, but I end up tipping my head back and doing it. She's gathered thick spit on her tongue and lets it slowly drip into my mouth. It's not much, but it makes me crazy. I can't explain why I like the things I do, and it's hard to find a partner who's willing to play in all the ways I like. Until Mak came into my life.

"Swallow like a good boy," she says in a sultry voice.

I obey.

Mak impales herself on my cock over and over, squatting down on me like I'm a toy for her to play with. I lay back and enjoy every second of being dominated like this. But when her legs start to shake and her rhythm is lost, I take control and thrust my hips upwards again and again while holding her hips to keep her in place.

She claws my biceps and I hope she draws blood.

Rolling her over, I hook my elbows under her legs, and lift her higher to rail her at a new, tilted angle.

She gasps.

I stop. "Too much?"

"N-no."

I don't believe her. "Mak, is it too deep?" I test her out, driving into her slower this time, and her breath hitches again. I stop and arch my brow, waiting for her to speak.

"I like it. But go slow until I say otherwise."

No problem. "What's your safe word?"

"Cupcake."

"Good girl." I thrust slowly, holding my breath while I do because her inner walls clamp down on my dick with a vice grip. "Play with your clit for me."

She licks her middle finger and brings it down between her legs. The sight of my cock coated in her cream, her pussy wrapped around my base, and her slender fingers rubbing circles around her clit—it's a concoction heady enough to make me dizzy with need. I want to fill her to the brim and collar her for good.

"Faster," she says, her voice raspy. "I want it hard when I come on your big dick."

This woman is perfection.

I give her what she asks for, keeping my attention locked on her body language and the noises flying out of her pretty little mouth. My balls draw tight again.

"I'm close," she rasps.

Our bodies slap together. Sweat blooms down my back. My grip tightens on her legs and when she lets out a glorious scream, her pussy clenches around me and milks my cock, kicking me over the edge with her. I roar my release, and I empty myself for a second time in my girl.

Pulling out, I stare at her pussy, loving how my cum drips out of her.

I wish I could take a picture of this to keep forever.

"Holy smokes," Mak says panting, with her arms draped over her chest. "My heart's racing so fast."

That makes two of us, only mine isn't from the cardio.

Chapter 22

Mak

This is exactly what I needed—a hard fuck with a hot guy, followed by snacks and cuddle time. Laying against Carson makes me wonder why I never cuddled before. My other relationships were not like this one. We rarely took time to appreciate each other in simple ways like I do with Carson.

I've always been on a tight schedule with a million things on my plate, so snuggling up afterwards was never a thing for me. I've always been more of a hit it and split it girl.

But with Carson, it's different. He wipes all responsibility from my mind. All I want to do is stay wrapped in his arms. Every time we're together, I find it hard to pull away from him afterwards. It's ironic that he and I aren't in this for the long haul. Maybe having a contractual arrangement has taken the pressure off of us and that's why it's so nice.

Carson kisses the top of my head while we watch a movie on my laptop. My second wind has died down, and my eyes are lead weights that finally close for good.

When I wake up, Carson's arm is wrapped around my waist like a bar on a roller coaster. I'm not sure how I'll ever slip out. His light snoring is adorable. Wonder if I can wake him up with a little butt wiggle?

I try with zero success. Closing my eyes again, I drift back off to sleep.

When I wake a second time, my right leg and arm are sprawled across his body as if I'm pinning him down. Maybe, subconsciously, I was. I keep dreading the possibility of waking up and him having already slipped away to head back home.

His head is tipped away from me and he's still out like a light. Holy mother of hotness, Carson's sexy even when he sleeps. His pitch-black hair is all tussled and half in his face. His bottom lip is pushed out a little further than the top, making him look so damn kissable. His body takes up more than half my queen-sized bed and his feet actually hang off the edge. With just a blanket draped over his groin, I wonder if he kicked all the covers off in the middle of the night. This man is a furnace, which is another reason I probably slept so good.

Running a featherlight touch down his chest, I admire every inch of this man's body. He's soft and hard in all the right places. With him asleep, he doesn't flinch or tense up when I touch him. I can't understand why he seems to be uncomfortable whenever I run my hands all over him when we fuck, but I'm glad he hasn't told me to stop.

Gripping his hard dick, I pump it a couple times, wondering if he'll wake up or not.

He doesn't.

Okay, I need to stop creeping on him like this and get my ass in gear. Slinking out of the room, I snag my cell to check my messages. That's when I get an awful, wonderful, sneaky idea. Slipping back into my now bright bedroom, I crawl back into bed with Carson, and snap a couple pictures of us together snuggling. I don't know why I do it, but I love the way we look together.

We make a really pretty couple.

He breathes in deep and then stretches out like a huge cat. "Morning, Beautiful."

Crawling on top of him, I flash a huge, cheesy grin. I'm not normally so energetic when I wake up, but with Carson's eyes on me like this, a boost of adrenaline shoots through me. I can't remember the last time I've been this happy. "Good morning, sleepyhead."

"There's nothing good about mornings, weirdo." He yawns and rubs the sleep from his eyes.

"Really?" Sliding down his body, I lick his hard cock and start sucking it.

"Mmmph." His hand dives into my messy hair and holds a hunk of it. "I take it back.

Happy best, good, wonderful morning to you, too."

I laugh with his dick in my mouth. It makes him groan.

So I do it again.

"Your mouth feels so good on me." His hips slowly raise so he can fuck my face. It's gentle and yet not. I love it. Hollowing my cheeks, I suck him off while stroking his shaft and I grab his balls with my freehand. His breaths turn ragged a few seconds later. "Swallow me. I want you to drink every motherfucking drop I have for you."

That's all the warning I have before he explodes in my mouth. It's salty and sweet and I make sure to drain him dry before popping off and licking my now swollen lips. I love how he looks at me. I love how fast I can make him unravel. I love that he's breathing hard because of what I did to him. And I love how our energies always seem to match.

"You keep doing things like this and I'm going to put a collar on your pretty neck."

I assume he's joking, which is the only reason I don't get my hopes up. Before I overthink it, I switch topics. "Got any photo sessions today?"

"No. This is an editing day. I have a lot of admin work to do too. Plus, I have to hunt down some models for book covers and work on my social media. What about you?"

It takes me a moment to respond. He sounds busy, and I was kind of hoping he wouldn't be. Damnit. "I'm off today and want to do nothing but read." *And be with you...* I don't say that part. The last thing I want is to sound like a needy woman who can't be without her sexy, kinky guy for a day.

Carson nods before sitting up and scooching out of my bed. Grabbing his boxer briefs off the floor, he tugs them back on and reaches for his jeans next. "I should get going."

My heart drops. I don't want him to go yet. Will I sound desperate if I ask him to stay?

"Mind if I use your bathroom real quick?"

"No. Sure. Go ahead." It'll give me time to recollect myself.

Stupid, Mak. Why don't you offer him breakfast or ask if he wants to go out later.

While the faucet runs in my bathroom, I quickly throw on some comfy sweats and pull my hair into a messy bun. Carson comes out just as I'm pulling down my sweatshirt that says, "Buy me books and tell me to STFUATTDLAGG."

He freezes and reads my shirt. Looks me in the eyes. Narrows his gaze back on my shirt and then arches his eyebrow. A knowing smile slides across his face.

"Nice shirt."

"Thanks." I smooth it over my chest. "Want pancakes? Eggs? Bacon?"

Hesitation flickers across his face. "No. I probably shouldn't." The clanking of his belt buckle sounds loud in my otherwise quiet room while he pulls his jeans on. "What are you reading today?"

"Umm. I have some arcs to finish and a buttload of reviews to post. My bookstagram account needs some attention. I've been working so much, I haven't had time to do anything with it."

It never came up in conversation, so I don't think he knew I was a bookstagrammer.

"That's cool." He snatches his ripped t-shirt from the floor and we both stare at it. Oh no, he can't wear that thing home, it's ruined! Without saying a word, he tosses it into the trash and shrugs at me as if saying "oh well." But there's something sad in his eyes, too.

His movements are all stiff and confusing again. He kind of reminds me of a trapped animal that can't figure a way out.

So I make it easy for him. "Thanks for last night." I leave my bedroom first, hoping he'll follow me out.

And praying he doesn't.

"No problem. Thanks for this morning." Carson grabs his cell from his back pocket and checks it. His brow digs down for a second, then he pockets the damn thing again. "Enjoy your books." He heads to the door, and I want to scream for him to stop. I feel like something's changed and I can't, for the life of me, figure out what it is.

But something's wrong. Really wrong.

Panic puts me in a chokehold and all my words get caught in my throat.

Carson pulls open the door and braces against it, as if struggling on whether to stay or go. "If you want to stop by later, I can order takeout. I'll be at the studio most of the day, but should be home around seven."

I gulp past the lump lodged in my aching throat. "Umm. Yeah. Maybe. Sure."

His broad, bare back tenses, all his muscles and taut skin flex, and then I hear the sound of a woman and two kids running down the hall and a door slamming shut. After that, Carson's shoulders sag and he nods again. Without looking back at me, he steps outside and shuts the door behind him.

I don't know why, but tears spring to my eyes.

A moment ticks by. Then two. Then three. Looking out my window, my knees feel weak as I watch him get into his car. Turning away, I suck in deep breaths. What on earth just happened between us? What's happening to *me*?

I don't understand why I feel any of the emotions I keep having around this man. Turning away, I swipe the tears from my cheeks, determined not to let myself fall to pieces over something this silly.

Someone pounds loudly on my door, scaring me half to death. I don't know who that could be, but I'm praying it's not my neighbor two doors down. She's annoying and always wants to complain about the landlord. Gathering my composure, I swing the door open.

Carson stands before me, his bare chest rising and falling like he just ran up both flights of steps. I don't get a chance to ask why he's back. He cups my face and smashes his mouth to mine in a kiss that steals the air from my lungs and cells out of my brain.

When he pulls away, he says, "Pack your books, pretty girl."

I don't give him time to change his mind.

Chapter 23

Carson

They say the bigger they are, the harder they fall. I'm falling like a comet through the sky and when I hit bottom, the hole I'll make will be catastrophically massive.

I'm not in love with Mak. I keep telling myself that because, even if it feels close, it's not the same as what I felt with Lauren. No, this is just infatuation. Instalust at best. We play well together and she's so sweet and nothing like my normal subs that I'm fooling myself into believing she's just a fun twist on an old favorite game.

And I'll keep lying to myself for as long as I have to because this will never grow into something beyond a kink app hookup. I've had so many, I know the drill. And the fact that I make sure my subs know that this is all play, and not reality, is a real kick in the balls now that I'm having to remind myself that's all this is with Mak.

But I couldn't leave her this morning. I tried. Something went off the rails between us earlier and it's me.

I'm the problem.

I'm always the fucking problem.

My derailment happened when I realized my shirt couldn't be salvaged. I was going to have to walk out of this apartment complex bare chested. It shouldn't have mattered. And at first, it almost didn't. But then that woman came out with her two kids and my insecurity demons roared to life with a vengeance to tear me down.

I'm a grown ass man. I've been shirtless in front of people tons of times. I get through it just fine because I'm with family and friends and I feel safe and comfortable with them.

This building is not my safe space.

I felt vulnerable and exposed. Those are two things I don't do. Ever.

Last night, Mak said I was sexy. I didn't take it to heart because lots of people say things in the heat of the moment to make their partner feel good. But in the back of my mind, I can't really believe she'd think that was the truth. I saw her ex-boyfriend. Motherfucker looked like Superman.

I feel more like Wreck It Ralph.

When I barreled out of the apartment complex and got into my car, I felt stupid. Why should I let my past destroy this morning? Why did I allow myself to go into a dark headspace and walk away from Mak's bright sunshine? I thought I was better than this by now. All the work I've put into myself seems to have dissolved. I've got to try harder.

Mak deserves better.

I'm getting attached to her and it's scaring me.

That comment I made earlier about putting a collar around her neck? I hadn't meant for that to slip out. But it's the truth. I want to keep her.

And I can't.

She'll play with me and then move on to another partner with more to offer, and that's exactly how it should be. It's one of the reasons I'm on that site and in this lifestyle—I get to embrace my kinks with willing partners, and there's no commitment beyond what we initially agree on.

Lots of Doms don't word their contracts like I do. I handle it more like a service rendered. That's it. No harm, no foul, no hard feelings... no broken hearts.

But my heart cracked when I felt Mak's gaze burning into my back just before I left her apartment. And by the time I made it to my car, I knew I had to make a choice. Drive off and pretend this is okay or break another motherfucking rule and do what I'm doing now.

"Pack your books, pretty girl."

My lips are still tingling from the hard and violent kiss we just shared. Mak's eyes round with excitement, and... I think relief... as she snatches a stack of books over by her couch and unplugs her e-reader from the end table.

"I ummm…" Mak pivots on her bare feet and looks around her apartment. "Snacks?"

"Anything you want." I'll order delivery for lunch and make us dinner at home tonight, if she'll let me keep her that long. "Shoes," I say, when she runs up with her arms filled with a huge stack of paperbacks.

"Hold these for me?" She dumps them into my arms and dashes to her bedroom. I can't help but smile. She seems genuinely excited to be stuck with me for the day. "Here…" She hops on one foot while trying to adjust her Chucks. "I got a bag."

"Slow down, Mak." It's not like the place is on fire. "Take a minute and tie your shoes."

She falls on her ass and laces her Chucks up properly, which makes me happy because I don't need her tripping on the steps and breaking her sweet body. Meanwhile, I shove all the books into her bag. There's no way she's reading all these in a day, so I'm assuming they're for her Instagram posts, but what do I know.

"Want me to follow you?" she asks while locking her door.

"How about you just ride with me? I'll head home to change and then we can go to the studio."

"Okay."

The tension and awkwardness I felt leaving

her the first time has blown to bits. We're right back to being perfectly happy and comfortable again.

God help me, I'm in so much trouble with this one…

• • •

Mak's a beautiful distraction. I put my playlist on shuffle mode and it's giving my emotions whiplash. Songs bounce from Bad Omens, Eminem, Dolly Parton, Korn, to Sam Tinnesz.

One of the nice things about letting my clients choose the music during their sessions is I've been introduced to a lot of artists I might not have heard of otherwise. I've got one hell of an eclectic compilation rocking through my studio because of it.

Mak seems to know the words to just about every song that plays. That throws me a little. For someone who's into Blackpink, the woman hasn't skipped a beat no matter what song plays next and hardly any of it has been K-Pop.

I try my best to concentrate on my projects but all I really do is constantly sneak glances at her while she uses all my props to set up little scenes for her books to make posts with. Right now, she's standing on top of a table with a collection of plastic flowers and candles scattered around a hardback.

Unable to take it anymore, I get up and walk over and hold her hips. "I'm scared you're going to fall."

She growls with frustration. "Ugh! I keep casting a shadow over my stuff. I keep trying to reposition myself, but nothing's working. I always have this problem."

Lifting her off the chair, she squeals. "Let me help?"

"Okay."

Snagging a light and some filters, I do a little quick rearranging. "How's that?"

"You're amazing." She holds her phone out and snaps a few pics at ground level.

"Want to use my camera? The quality will be better, and I can just drop them onto your cell."

She chews her bottom lip and debates it. "Okay. Yeah. Thanks."

I'm thrilled, honestly. I like sharing my space and skills with her. I just want to make sure I don't take over her project because I tend to do that sometimes. Getting her all set up, I show her how to use one of my cameras, then go back to my desk to work.

But not before busting out some moves to *Work It* by Missy Elliott.

"Ohhhh!" Mak joins in and pops her ass to the beat. "Get it, boy!" She goes down low.

I one up her by going down even lower.

She squeals with delight and claps her

hands, hyping me up. I forget that I'm supposed to be working and just let myself have some fun.

Hey, just because I don't know line dances doesn't mean I can't drop it like it's hot.

Mak dances around, laughing and singing, then she presses up against me from behind. Running her nails down my back, we bump and grind like two fools with no cares in the world. I momentarily falter when Mak snakes her hands across my front to hold me against her.

Grabbing her hands, I spin around and kiss her knuckles. My heart's pounding a mile a minute. "Get back to work, woman!" She giggles when I smack her ass playfully and sets back on her mission to make the best Instagram book posts while I drop back into my chair and rub my aching chest.

It feels good to be around Mak. I haven't been my goofy self with someone in a long time. But damn, that was a close one. I wasn't expecting her to full on grip my goddamn love handles like that.

Metal scrapes across the floor as she drags more stuff around and takes full advantage of my studio to make her book pics look amazing. This place is big enough for us to be in each other's presence without necessarily being in each other's space, if that makes any sense.

I turn the music down a little so I can concentrate. "You hungry yet?"

"No!" she calls out. "But if you are, order

something. Don't wait for me."

I can hold off.

Editing more photos, I finish up the three clients I had left from last week and shoot the galleries over through email, including Mak's. "Just sent you your pics."

She's at my chair so fast, I didn't hear her approach. "Ohhh! They're done? Let me see!"

I pull her onto my lap. "Here you go."

I sit back and hold her hips, rubbing my thumbs on her lower back while she clicks on her gallery. "Oh wow, Carson." She clicks some more. "Holy crap." She clicks some more. "I look so hot."

"You are so hot."

"No. I look like a goblin most of the time. But these…" She shakes her head and clicks back to one of her with a book between her legs, her fingers spreading the pages as if they're something else between her thighs she's fingering. "I could cry."

It's not uncommon for a client to see themselves one way and then I take their photos and capture them in a different view. It's rewarding for me, and a confidence boost for them.

Ironic, right, considering I have the worst body dysmorphia ever.

But that's why I got into this business. I don't want anyone to feel the way I do about myself. If I can show them a new perspective, then they'll know how truly gorgeous they are.

Mak's a natural born man killer. And when she turns around and kisses me, that's natural too. "Mak, I want to ask you something, and you can totally say no."

"I'll say yes."

"Hear me out first."

"Yes."

Growling, I narrow my gaze and try to act mad even though I'm fighting to not laugh. "What do you say to modeling in the tub for me?"

She stiffens in my lap. "Like nudes for your portfolio?"

"Uh no." I cringe. "For a book cover."

Her eyes grow to the size of dinner plates. "Are you *serious*, Carson?"

"Yeah. I need a model and the more I think about it, the more I'm convinced you would be perfect. It's a high fantasy thing with nature and water."

"This is the Florence and the Machine inspired thingy Trey talked about the other night?"

"Yeah." I can't believe she remembers that. "You want to give it a shot?"

"Hells YES!" Mak hops off my lap. "This is wild!" She practically skips over to the tub and claps her hands, jumping up and down. "I don't even care if the author ends up changing their mind. Just doing this is so cool. I can't believe

I'm about to be a book cover model."

Her excitement makes my cheeks hurt from the smile I'm rocking. "Grab all the flowers you can find."

If the plastic ones don't work, I'll go down the street and buy a bunch of fresh ones from the florist, but I suspect what I already have will be perfect.

The whole setup takes me over an hour to arrange. "I think we're ready." I hunt down my camera and pause as Mak strips out of her clothes. The studio doors are locked, so we're not in jeopardy of anyone crashing the shoot. She's safe here with me.

Hozier starts singing over the speakers. That artist is a whole ass mood and I'm here for it with Mak and me doing this photoshoot. I should put on Florence and the Machine, but I'm not walking away from Mak now that she's naked in front of me.

"Ohhhh, it's nice and warm," she says, stepping into the tub with my help.

"Did you think I'd make it cold?"

"I'm still blown away that there's running water in this place. I thought this was just a prop, not an actual working tub. The water temp didn't register until I put my foot in."

I straddle the rim of the bathtub to take photo after photo of my gorgeous girl. There's a chain above me I can hold on to, so I don't accidentally fall in and crush her to death, but

I'm poised like a panther and don't have trouble with my balance.

Mak's hair spreads in the water, filling in the spots the flowers don't. She's wearing bare minimum makeup on her lips and eyes, courtesy of Chloe's insanely huge stash of makeup. We reshoot over and over, adding and taking away different details. We switch out the flowers. I color the water. We add fog from a machine I have. Bubbles. Candles. Reflections. By the end of it, I have more photos for Trey to pull from than all my book cover sessions combined. It's overkill, I know, but I can't stop clicking shot after shot. Mak's loving this as much as I am and my heart swells seeing her this happy.

"I think we're done." I help her out of the tub and hand her a towel. "You were amazing."

"So were you." She dries off her body before wrapping her hair up in the same towel.

My dick's been rock hard the entire time. It hurts like a sonofabitch, trapped in my jeans.

"Do you ever take pics of yourself?" she asks.

"No." Why would I?

"Do you ever take them with your play partners?"

I feel like she's setting up a trap. "I've taken pics of my subs. But never us together. Why?"

She shrugs and looks over at the bed. "Want to take some with me?"

My dick goes limp. "Why?"

Mak saunters over and pokes my chest. "For my spank bank, silly."

She told me she got off on my profile pic last night, but that was with a picture of my face. Not my whole ass body. My knee-jerk reaction is to deny her request, but I stall out.

Do better. She deserves it.

Maybe this will be good for me. Good for *us.* "If you want to… sure."

Mak crosses her arms over her chest. "That didn't sound very enthusiastic."

My brain's scrambling. She's naked and asking me to give her something I'm perfectly capable of. I just… need to work up the nerve first.

Setting up three tripods, I take longer than necessary to look for the remote for one camera and adjust my settings on another. I also grab her cell and set it on video record so I can snag some pics off that too. All this is to make the scene as best as possible, but it's also a time sucker so I can gather my confidence enough to do this for her.

The filters are in place, and the lighting is perfect, which now means I've got nothing else left to use as an excuse. "Ready?"

"Yyyyup." She's already on the bed naked, with her wet hair falling around her shoulders. "Get over here, hot stuff."

My face burns as I pull off my shirt and

drop it like it's covered in fire ants. I don't feel good. My stomach's twisting in knots.

Mak crawls back to give me room on the bed. "You're keeping your pants on?"

"For now." I'm actually really proud of my ass and thighs, hell, even my arms. It's just my gut that's got me all fucked in the head and that's what is exposed right now. I need to work on this for myself, and now is my chance. I just have to take this moment in baby steps.

"Get over here, Big Boy." The cameras are rolling. Mak giggles and lifts on her knees so we can kiss. Her chilled fingers roam up my arms and down my chest. She pulls on my belt buckle, making me thrust forward a little.

That makes me growl. "You can't just go yanking on a man's belt, woman. It turns us feral."

She yanks me again.

I growl again.

We start kissing and soon, I'm taking charge. I hold her in various embraces, knowing what's best for this angle, and keep my movements slow so the cameras have time to capture it.

"Crawl in front of me," I order. Mak does as she's told and my dick's hard again, and still stuffed in jeans that are way too tight and hot. "Wrap your arms around my neck and look at the camera."

I kiss the side of her neck and sprawl my

fingers out on her lower belly like she's a possession of mine.

"This feels so sexy, Carson."

I can't agree or disagree. My head is stuck between enjoying the moment and masking myself.

"Wait!" She crawls away and comes back with a leather crop from my BDSM props. "Can I play with this?"

"Sure."

"Strip."

Fuck. I slowly unlace my boots and kick them off. Then I work on getting out of my jeans.

This is for her, I keep reminding myself. She's turned on, that's obvious, but I'm nervous as hell about how far this will go and how I'll feel about it later.

"So. Damn. Sexy." Mak playfully bites the leather crop and growls like a baby wolf.

I respond with a deeper, louder growl of my own. "How about I use this on you first, little beastie?"

I instinctively grab a third camera that's for close shots and have Mak lie on her belly. Running the riding crop down her spine, I snap off several pics. The *click, click, click* of the cameras fill my ears. Straddling her thighs, I tap her ass with the riding crop and she yelps.

"Too hard?"

"No, but I don't think I like it."

I toss the crop over my shoulder and kiss

the blooming red mark to make it better.

"Well, I do like that," she says when I kiss her butt cheek again.

"Oh yeah, and how about this?" I nip her flesh.

"Mmm hmm."

"Aaaand, this?" I sink a finger into her pussy and find her soaked. "I think I have my answer already."

Click, click, click, click…

The cameras are still going, and I reign myself in. We're not at a point in our relationship to have a porn film made. It's already pushing my lines taking these photos. Crawling off the bed, I snatch my shirt and quickly put it back on. Then I stop the equipment and notice Mak's watching me. She looks confused and disappointed. "You good?"

"I wanted us *both* naked," she pouts.

"You can have me naked at home." I toss her a wink. "How about tonight I cook dinner and feed you in my lap while you read me word porn?"

"You're like, the hottest, greatest guy on the planet." Her pouty face vanishes, replaced by a huge smile that warms me from the inside out. "How much more work do you have left?"

"I'm done for the day, if you are."

"I'm done too." She gets dressed while I break down the scene and put my cameras away. "Carson?"

"Yeah?" I collapse the tripods and tuck them under my arm.

"Thanks for doing that with me."

I gulp. "No problem."

She's suddenly at my back again, and her hands feel like ice when she touches me under my shirt. "I can tell you didn't want to do that shoot."

The dejection in her tone cuts me deep. "Yes, I did. I wouldn't have done it unless I wanted to, Mak." It's only a half lie.

But now I've broken another rule of mine. The second most important one—Always be open and honest.

Chapter 24

Mak

Something is up with Carson. Ever since this morning, he's been running hot and cold. It makes my stomach squirm because I realize how much I don't know about him. We just sort of crashed into each other on that kink app and there are moments where I feel like I'm blurring lines between the Dom/sub dynamic I thought we were in, and an actual relationship that I wish we were in.

It's not all on me. He's the one who keeps inviting me places. I've just been all too eager to stay with him for as long as possible and don't tell him no.

We click. I like it. I like being around him. I like how much we laugh and get along. I'm more myself around him than I am around most of the people in my life, except for Leah. I know it's too soon to call this more than infatuation, but other words for what I feel when I'm around Carson hang on the tip of my tongue. And they're big words with big feels.

I could easily fall in love with this guy.

He's sweet, caring, observant, fun, successful, and hot as sin.

I feel connected to him, except I don't know him at all. I'm only going off how I feel when I'm in his space. That's not okay. It's confusing and scary. It's *dangerous*. My heart is getting closer and closer to being put on the line, and I don't know what I'll do if he ends this soon.

Part of me suspects he's got similar concerns. Carson keeps putting walls up, whether he realizes it or not, and I have no clue why or what for. Should I ask? Should I point out that his body language is different when I touch him in certain ways? Should I bring up my feelings? Should I tell him to just take me home now so he's not obligated to do it later?

His forearm flexes on the steering wheel while he drives with one hand, the other rests on my thigh. There's a stack of leather bracelets and one beaded one on his wrist, all black. I like that he's touching me in a semi-possessive way. Placing my hand over his, I entwine our fingers together, taking note of how small mine are compared to his. I love how we look together. How we fuck together. How we dance and laugh and eat and chill out together.

"You okay?" I can't stop worrying that this will end too soon.

Carson flicks his gaze at me. "Yeah, you?"

"Yeah." It's not a lie. "I just feel like…" I

stop myself from saying more as he pulls onto his street.

"You feel like what, Mak?"

My belly squirms again. "I'm hungry." What a cop-out and a half. I don't want to admit that I can't understand what's going on between us. Maybe I'm just reading into things and overthinking too much.

"Do you like chicken enchiladas?"

"Love them."

A smile bursts across his face as he pulls into his driveway. "Then that's what we'll have for dinner."

Some of the tightness in my chest eases as we enter his home. It smells like vanilla cake in here and I love it. Carson drops his camera bag on the couch and tells me to sit back and get comfortable while he heads to the kitchen. "Want some help?"

"No, I want you to just relax. It won't take me long."

"Okay." Pulling out my phone, I check my notifications on Instagram first. I'm not a big bookstagrammer by any means, but I love making posts and hyping authors up. With all the photos I took today, I'm hoping it'll gain me more followers because they are absolute fire. I was spoiled today with all of Carson's equipment and props. How will I ever go back to my regular book photos after this?

I open up my albums to grab the first

photo to post on Insta and freeze when I see the video of Carson and I posing on the bed. Tapping it, I watch with my mouth watering. Damn, we look so good together. His hands are all over me, hungry and possessive. His dark hair falls into his eyes when he bends down to nip my shoulder.

I swallow hard, my pussy getting wet as I keep watching us together.

Click. I screenshot part of the video. *Click, click.* I keep doing it. Each pic is hotter than the last. Blowing one up, I crop it, and mess with the light exposure. I'm by no means a professional photographer like Carson, but I'm pretty handy with the filters on my phone.

"Wowwy zowwy." We make a really hot couple.

Wait. Is that what we are? What do you call this dynamic? Does it even have a title?

I feel him before I see him behind me. Grinning hard, I lift my cell to show him a banging picture of the two of us I just screenshot. "We look insanely hot together, don't we?"

Carson looks at the photo, then at me, then at the screen again. His face turns beet red. His jaw ticks when he clenches his teeth.

Oh no. I've overstepped a line I didn't realize was there. "I'll delete them if you want me to. I…"

He shakes his head and turns away, but I

quickly grab his arm. "Carson." He yanks out of my flimsy grip. Anger and frustration flare inside me. "What's wrong?"

I don't sound as concerned as I do mad.

"Nothing." He storms back into the kitchen, leaving me two choices: follow or stay.

It takes me a little too long to decide and by then, my heart's jack hammering. This is not how two grown adults act. Tearing into the kitchen, I've got a million arguments ready to fire while he has his back to me and is chopping cilantro.

"What's going on with you, Carson? You've been acting hot and cold ever since this morning."

He drops the knife on the cutting board with a clank. "I know."

Okay then, glad he's self-aware. "Why?" Hands on my hips, I silently will him to turn around and face me. He doesn't. "I don't understand what's going on."

His shoulders sag and voice is gruff when he says, "I know." He slowly turns around and leans against the counter with his arms crossed over his chest.

It's the universal body language for *leave me alone*.

"Talk to me," I practically beg. "If I've done something wrong or crossed a line…" Reaching out, I try to touch him.

He moves away. "Don't touch me right

now."

I freeze.

Then I back up.

Our dynamic requires trust and honesty and openness. He's not living up to his end of the contract. "Tell me something," I whisper. "*Please*. I don't understand what's happening here."

I should have known this was too perfect. It was just an act. The classic be-on-your-best-behavior-in-the-beginning-of-a-relationship bullshit. Carson's mask has apparently dropped, and I'm now staring at a very different man.

It makes me want to cry. Tears prick my eyes, but I refuse to let them go.

He won't open his mouth to speak. Staring at me with these big brown eyes, his chest expands and contracts while he breathes harder, faster, as if he's trying to stop all his emotions from leaking out at once. That's what scares me most. He's on the verge of breaking and I don't get why.

My voice shakes as I try to remain calm. "I'll erase the video and pictures." Pulling my cell out again, I tap the screen to get started.

"No." He places his hand over my cell, covering up the picture of us, and takes it from me.

My hackles raise. "Carson, give me my phone back."

He stares at me for a heartbeat, then his

gaze falls to the photos I've screenshot. It's all I can do to not rip my cell phone out of his hand, but seeing his expression makes me hesitate. He looks *devastated.*

Why?

Chapter 25

Carson

Every single photo she's captured seems to highlight everything I hate about myself.

It's not Mak's fault that I feel this way. My own hangups are always poking and prodding my confidence, and today's session in the studio gave them new weapons to beat me down with.

I've been with my fair share of women, all shapes and sizes, but not once have I been with someone like Mak. She's so petite and spunky and fun and sweet and oblivious to how different we really are. It makes me want to call things off with her and also keep her forever.

"Carson?" Her sweet, soft voice trembles and it makes me feel worse.

I should just hand over my man card and sit in time out since I'm behaving like a child.

"I don't know what you see in this video or these pictures, but..." I expand one, homing in on the way my belly rolls over my belt. "I can't stand the sight of myself."

The air is vacuumed out of the kitchen. I can't breathe. I can't move. I can't look at Mak.

"What?" her voice cracks. "Carson, how can you say that?"

Easy. Just look at my picture. "I've worked really hard on my body for the better part of ten years. It's never enough. I'm… never going to be enough."

The oven beeps, signaling it's time to put the tray of enchiladas I'd made up yesterday into the oven to bake. "You deserve someone better than me," I choke out. "Someone who matches you better than I do."

Mak scoffs. "We're not a pair of socks. We match perfectly as is."

She's right on the first, but not the second statement. "Look at me." I smack my stomach, and it jiggles.

"Look at me!" she screams right back and smacks her belly too. "What the hell are you expecting, Carson? Six-pack abs?"

For all the work I put in at the gym? Damn right, I do. But all I have are flabs that mock me every time I do sit-ups. "You don't get it."

"Try me." She's fuming and I swear even our tempers match. Mak crosses her arms over her chest, just like me. "Go ahead. Let's hear it."

Fine. Here it comes, pretty girl. She's going to run out my door by the time I'm done trauma dumping on her.

"I'm going to wager a guess and say you don't know what it's like to be a fat kid. I used to have people poke my belly and call me the

Pillsbury Doughboy all the time. Instead of crying, I'd laugh like that stupid commercial character and let them poke me all the time because I thought I'd win them over with my humor. Spoiler Alert: I didn't."

Her brows knit together.

"Bet you didn't get picked last for teams at gym either." I can't believe I'm dragging all this history up. It's stupid and unfair and not okay. "Bet you didn't get shot down by every girl in the school. Bet you didn't get trays of nachos and French fries thrown at you in the cafeteria while they made pig noises. Bet you weren't called a fat ass, and blubber flubber, and a whale during swim class."

Tears fill her eyes and her chin trembles. I fucking hate it.

"Bet no one made you believe you were going to prom with the only girl who would talk to you in Chemistry, only to find out it was on a dare and she was paid to say yes and then when you showed up with the limo you rented, and the perfect corsage you spent hours agonizing over, she was standing in her living room taking pictures with her real date. And when they opened the door to leave, they walked right by you like you *didn't fucking exist*."

Mak's hands drop to her sides as the air rushes out of her.

"Bet you didn't get into the Dom lifestyle because it was the only way to have control over someone touching you intimately."

Her face turns red.

"Bet you…" Fuck. "Bet you didn't…" My heart's slamming in my chest and I feel like I'm sinking into the floor. "Bet you didn't fall in love and have her scream in your face that you weren't enough. That you'll never be enough. And then, while you're on your knees begging her to stay, she cuts off the symbol of your relationship and throws it in your face like trash. Like *you're* trash. Like you're not worth being in love with because you're… not… you're not enough. When the reality is… I'm too much."

My head falls and I can't believe I just fucking did this.

Mak should run out my front door and never look back.

I just broke my number one rule: I cracked open and let someone see the real, no good, pathetic, messed up me.

Rage and embarrassment swarm me. My cheeks grow numb and I can't feel my fucking feet. "I know you didn't mean anything bad when you asked me to do a couples shoot today. But…" I shake my head and blow out a long, shaky breath. "All I see is how perfect you are, and how I'm not built to deserve you."

"Oh, Carson." Tears fall down her cheeks. It's my fault. I'm a deranged fuck with no self-esteem, and I've let my insecurities affect her. Before I have the sense to stop myself, I'm taking steps to close the gap between us and swipe the tears from her cheeks. I hate that I've made her cry. I hate that she's staring at me with pity.

I hate everything about myself.

All my life, I've had to mask my feelings and fit into some socially acceptable box. I turned into the funny one. The loud one. The obnoxious one, if the occasion called for it. That's how I survived high school and college. Then I grew the fuck up and got help and worked out all the time to lose weight and what's left just won't go away. I was forced to admit that I'll never be like the men on the covers of romance novels. I'll never be perfect.

Maybe that makes me sound like a little whiny bitch, but I don't give a fuck. It's how I feel. I've always felt bad about myself. All my friends were cut and didn't have an ounce of body fat on them. It's hard to get a date when your buddies are stacked and jacked while you look like a teddy bear.

I've always been friend-zoned.

Whenever I did manage to get a girl to be with me—which wasn't until college—I'd spoiled her rotten in fear of her kicking me to the curb for someone better looking than I was. I got taken advantage of time and time again until I learned to stop breaking myself just so a woman would welcome me to her bed.

That day when I took pictures of my girlfriend—who three weeks later dumped my ass and said we were better as friends, by the way—and she'd seen what I was able to capture and fell in love with herself? Fuck, I was so envious. I wanted to be able to look at myself like that too. But it hasn't happened. I can't look in the mirror and see anything other than my flaws. Pictures make it worse. I have no good angles.

Being a photographer was my greatest gift, and biggest curse. I may have found my calling, but there's always a barrier between me and everyone else. It's awful.

I have needs like every other hot-blooded person out there and I love women. All sizes. All shapes. All flavors. Becoming a Dom let me call the shots and also gave me a false sense of control. Keeping the dynamic strictly "business" was how I've survived with my heart intact.

Until Lauren.

After her, things changed. For better, for worse, I don't have a clue. But I refuse to tailor myself to fit someone else's mold like I used to. And I promised myself to *never* get my heart caught in a woman's claws again.

It's obvious that I've failed because Mak's got my heart in her hands right now.

I might have survived Lauren, but I don't know if I'll survive Mak. She makes me feel amazing and I'm not used to it. I don't like things I'm not used to.

"I'll call you an Uber," I say with a ragged,

defeated tone. "I'm sure you want to leave, and it's better if I'm not the one to take you home." My heart drops into the pit of my stomach. Pulling out my cell, I unlock the screen and open the app.

"I'm not going anywhere," she says, seething. "Put your phone down, Carson."

Our gazes lock and I'm rooted to the spot.

Mak walks up to me with her hands down at her sides, and she cranes her neck to look up at me. "It's my turn now."

Chapter 26

Mak

If he thinks he can just drop all that baggage on the ground between us and not expect me to have my say too, then he's a fool. My heart's broken for this man, but that doesn't mean I'll let him cast me out just so he can sulk.

We all have demons. We all have shitty history. We all have body image issues.

"It said in our contract that we have to be honest in all things." I want so badly to touch him, hug him, but it's clear he doesn't want that. The instant he wiped my tears away, he stepped back again. "So now I'm going to be super honest with you, Carson."

I clear my throat.

Okay, Mak. You can do this.

"I have a type." That's the lamest opening line ever. "I like big guys. I love how there's so much to touch and kiss and fuck."

"Yeah, I can tell," he huffs with indignation. "Your body builder ex probably has abs hard enough to chip a tooth on."

He does, but that's not the point. "I don't

care about his stupid abs. I didn't care about how often he went to the gym or what his BMI measurement was. That's not what attracted me to him. And it's not what attracts me to *you*."

I blow out a breath and try to focus on putting my feelings in order.

"Body dysmorphia is a hard thing to battle, Carson." I step closer. "And I'm so proud of you for working through some of your issues with it. I wish..." I hope I can articulate this right. "I wish you could see past what you consider flaws, so you can see what I do when I look at you." My throat feels like it's closing up. "It honestly hurts my feelings to hear you talk about yourself in bad ways. I think you're hot. I also think I have pretty good taste. I think we're perfect together and for the past couple of weeks I've been trying to wrap my head around the fact that there's going to come a point when our contract is up, and you'll move on to the next sub to train and play with."

Carson has the nerve to shake his head, like that isn't bound to happen.

I raise my hand. "Look, I'm not saying I'm in love with you. It's clear, just by this conversation, that I don't really know you all that well." My heart flops like a fish in my chest. "But I can easily see myself falling for you. It's... it's happening now as we stand here."

He makes a strained noise and drops his gaze from me.

"If what I'm about to say is off the mark, stop me, okay?" He nods and I continue. "You and I… we clicked right off the bat."

He nods.

"We're easy together. It takes no effort to have fun and be happy with each other, no matter what we're doing."

He nods again.

"We're new and this is scary."

He nods, but it's a little slower this time.

"We're crazy for each other."

He nods again, this time faster.

"I'm sexy as sin."

He lifts his gaze to meet mine and nods with a devilish smile on his face.

"*You're* sexy as sin."

He freezes.

I arch my brow and close the space between us, desperate to touch him, but still I refrain. "*I* think you're sexy as sin."

He gulps, then slowly nods.

Taking a chance, I pry his hands off his chest so I can hold them. "We're all built differently, Carson. What's one person's not enough, is another person's just right."

The redness in his cheeks has now spread down his neck.

I glance down at my feet. "Look how short I am. I'm probably an inch away from needing to use a booster seat in the car. Do you know how lucky you are that you can reach things on the top shelf? I have a step stool in my kitchen just to get my stupid peanut butter and I sometimes climb the grocery store shelves like a squirrel to reach the things I need."

He offers a little smile, as if what I just said was adorable.

"I'm totally disproportionate, in case that's escaped your notice." It's only a half-joke. "I have A minus cups, and a dump truck ass."

"There's no such thing as A minus cups."

"Lower case A's then."

"That's not a thing."

"Uh, yes, it is." Kind of, sort of, depends on who you talk to.

"I love your tits and your ass," he says in a deep voice.

"I love that you love them."

"And I love how tiny you are."

"Good." Because I stopped growing fifteen years ago.

"So far, I love everything about you, Mak."

"I'm glad." Running my fingertips up his chest, I raise up on my tiptoes and hook my arms around his neck. "I think we're a pretty amazing combo."

Wariness laces his voice. "I think so too."

"Good." I pull him down so our lips almost brush. "I want to worship every inch of your body, Carson. I'm sorry you've struggled with it your whole life, but... maybe, just *maybe*, if you're willing to let me, I can show you how fucking amazing it really is."

I feel him shut down again. His body stiffens and his gaze loses that hint of sparkle. "I don't think you can help."

"Will you let me try?"

He debates it for a few moments, then says, "Let me think about it."

●●●

As I give Carson a little space, we eat the best enchiladas I've ever had in my life. He said it was his secret recipe and if he tells me how to make it, he'll have to kill me.

"Death would be worth it. Holy crap, these are so good."

I've eaten five. Carson's had three.

"I make big batches and freeze them into single serving portions. You came just in time since I hadn't divided them out yet."

"Mmmph." I lick the sour cream off my bottom lip. "Hurray for my excellent timing. I love that for me."

There's still tension and vulnerability in the air between us, but that's okay. While we pretend that his breakdown didn't happen, I've been able to analyze and understand him so much better. "Can I ask you a question?"

He wipes his mouth off with a napkin. "Sure."

Carson hasn't really looked at me much

since he put the enchiladas in to bake. Sitting across from him, I'd hoped it would be better, but it's not. "What's the real reason you got into boudoir photography?" Because I don't think it was his girlfriend feeling great about herself like he originally told me.

He takes a big gulp of water then leans back in his chair, giving me full eye contact. "So others wouldn't feel the way I do."

That's what I figured. Carson's heart is so big, I don't know how it fits in his chest.

It makes me fall even harder for him.

"Was there ever a girlfriend who you took those pics of in college?"

"Yes." His brow furrows. "I didn't lie to you about that. But it's a secondary reason for why I chose this career. And it's also the reason I always give whenever someone asks me about it."

I nod.

"I think a lot of women pick apart their bodies and end up never seeing their beauty the way others do." He puts his hand up. "And yeah, I see the hypocrisy."

I don't say a word.

"But I also know that angles and lighting and poses can bring out the best and worst in a person's figure. For instance..." He gets up and takes his phone out to snap three selfies—one with the camera above his head, one front and center, and one with him looking down. He looks different in all of them. "It's all about knowing the right way to display yourself."

I get that. "Have you ever been turned off by a woman's physique before?"

He sits back down. "Nope."

"Liar."

Carson's brow digs down. "That's not a lie, Mak."

Bullshit. "You're telling me a woman's weight doesn't hinder your attraction of her?"

"I'm saying a woman's physique is not what gets me hard. It's their scent that does." He takes another bite of his food. "It's how I discovered primal play was even a thing. I went to a munch and finally got some answers that explained why I was attracted to certain things and then I did a lot of research on how to play safely with others. Being my size, and being this strong, I can easily hurt someone without meaning to. Plus, I know that it's intimidating to be the prey. I had to learn how to control myself while also keeping track of their body language and noises." He stuffs another bite of enchilada into his mouth and chews. "I never cared about their body type. I want their scent and their taste."

Holy shit, I'm wet just hearing him admit that.

"Am I the smallest woman you've been with?"

"Yes."

"Does that impact how you treat me?"

"Yes."

I feel insulted. "Don't treat me differently than your other subs. I have a safe word. I know how to use it."

"I know, Mak, but the last thing I want is to put you in a position where you *have* to use it. I was proud of you for saying it a few weeks ago, but that doesn't mean I want to keep pushing your boundaries over and over until you have to say it again. That's not how this dynamic works."

That's fair. "What's the craziest thing you've done with a partner?"

"Subjective," he says and takes a drink. "My crazy and your crazy might not align."

Interesting answer. "What's one thing you did that you'll never do again?"

He sits back and thinks about it. "I once let a woman peg me."

My eyes almost pop out of my head. "Really?" The image in my mind is... okay, it's hot.

He narrows his gaze and jabs his fork at me. "Don't get any ideas, Mak."

"I would never!" Yes, I would. "What didn't you like about it?"

"She was rough, and the pacing was all off. I've been with both men and women. I've been on the giving and receiving end, too. There's an art to getting fucked in the ass. That woman was trying to insert dominance in a very unpleasant and painful way."

Holy crap. "Was she your sub?"

"No. She was just someone I hooked up with. Her and her boyfriend wanted a third, and they picked me." He shrugs like it was no big deal. "I'm down for anything once. That was my once for pegging."

"You know…" I playfully run my hand along his tabletop. "I have experience with anal. I could spoon you and let you back that fine ass right up to my eagerly waiting strap on." I waggle my brows at him.

Carson bursts out laughing. "I should have known that was coming."

Some more of the tension dies down between us. I laugh, he laughs, and we settle back into comfortable silence. As I pick up our plates to bring to the sink, he stops me with his hand on my hips. Looking up at me from his chair, Carson's brown eyes are warm and lighter than they were earlier. "Thanks, Mak."

He's not talking about me washing the dishes.

But I'm worried he won't thank me for what I'm about to do.

Chapter 27

Carson

Mak has lured me up to my bedroom. She's up to something and I can't figure out what it is. When she asked me earlier if she could help me learn to love my body, I told her I'd think about it.

The truth is, it's all I think about. Mak touches me more than any other woman I've been with, and ever since our first contact, I've wondered what it would be like to relinquish control and let her have freedom over my body.

I feel safe with her.

But I've felt safe before and it didn't end well for me. I'm worried if I let my walls down again, I'll get hurt.

"Do you trust me, Carson?"

Loaded. Fucking. Question.

"Yes." So far.

And if whatever she's about to do breaks that trust, this is over between us. I'm too fragile for her to take advantage of right now, and the only reason I'm willing to play along is out of sheer morbid curiosity.

And because I'm a glutton for punishment.

And because I'm falling head over heels for her, and I really do trust her. Mak's seen the worst of me. The weak man under the façade of cut biceps, pecs, and ripped thighs.

She walks over to the wall of my toys and scans them as if she's about to pick out a few to use. We haven't negotiated terms for those things, but I'm willing to let her have fun with them if she wants. I'll guide her, so neither of us gets hurt. I love that she's adventurous. When I said I'll try anything once, I meant it.

I think Mak's very much the same way.

"Stand with the backs of your knees against the bed, Big Boy."

Big Boy. Not once has that term sounded insulting when it comes from her lips.

"Yes, ma'am."

Although I demand, and will assert, dominance in most situations, there have been a few occasions where I'll hand the keys to my kingdom over to another. It's been when I felt helpless and in need of grounding. To be thrown into a subspace that helps me deal with my life has been my go-to coping mechanism.

Big Boy, hot stuff, beast… she's called me several names as I have her. We never discussed honorifics. That's another glitch in my carefully constructed code with Mak. But it didn't seem to matter.

Damn, I've broken every fucking rule with this woman and look at where I am now.

At her mercy.

Under her scrutiny.

Enthralled by her.

"Do you know what I first noticed about you?" She gracefully walks over to me. "Your eyes. In your profile pic, your eyes caught my attention first. You always stare at me like a wolf would a rabbit. Your gaze makes me feel warm and adored."

I swallow hard, and don't say a word.

"The second thing I noticed was your mouth." She reaches up and drags her finger across my lips, pulling my bottom lip down a little before releasing it. "Such a gorgeous, lush, fuckable, kissable mouth you have."

Blood starts flowing to my cock.

"When I met you in person at my photo shoot, guess what part of your body caught my attention first."

I swallow again because my mouth's starting to water.

"Your ass." She leans over and spanks it. "Your ass is incredible. I want to bite it. Lick it. Scratch it all up."

Smiling, I let her keep talking.

"I imagined what it would look like, flexing as you fucked me."

Oh shit. My cock's harder now and bent the wrong way in my jeans. She unbuckles my belt and slides them down just enough to grab both ass cheeks and squeezes until her nails cut into my flesh.

Fuck. Yes. Please do more of this.

"Next, it was your forearms. I've never met a woman who wasn't a sucker for nice, thick, sinewy forearms, Carson. It's the universal weakness of our species." She drags her nails down my arms hard enough to leave red ribbons in her wake.

Mak appeals to my primal side, whether she means to or not. But what she does next makes me almost call it quits.

She plays with the hem of my shirt and lifts it up to expose my belly, but is too short to pull it off me. "Help me, please?" Her tone's half playful, half begging.

I reach around my back and yank it off. Shaking the hair out of my eyes, I watch her cautiously.

Mak bites her bottom lip and shimmies out of her pants.

That surprises me.

While her gaze roams all over my torso and lands on my belly button, she sinks her hand into her panties and groans. Pulling her fingers out, I can see them glistening from her arousal. Without saying a word, she runs her wet fingers across my mouth.

Her scent is unreal. Flicking my tongue across my lips, I get a taste of her and want to drop to my knees and shove my face in her sweet pussy. A growl tears out of me of its own accord.

While doing research and discovering

things about myself, I learned that I have an acute sense of smell. It's the reason I maintain light fragrances in my home and studio. I also never wear cologne and prefer my partners to not wear anything too perfume heavy.

Mak runs her hands up and down my chest again. "You're so big and strong. It makes me feel like you'll protect me from anything."

"I will." Shit, my voice hardly sounds like my own.

"I love your arms." She runs her hands down them again.

"They're perfect to hold you with," I say with a smile. What I should have said was to *keep* you with, because I don't think I'll ever be willing to let this woman go after today.

"And your thighs..." She yanks my jeans down until they pool around my ankles. I suck in a harsh breath when she claws down my legs, making goosebumps erupt on my skin.

"They're perfect for chasing you."

She looks up at me from the floor, her hazel eyes hooded with lust. Her face is right at my waistline. I hold my breath. Will she pull my boxers down next?

In silence, Mak runs her hands along my waistline—my greatest weakness, my worst character flaw, my kryptonite—and she kisses every soft inch of me.

I groan as my heart shatters and knees buckle. "Cupcake."

Chapter 28

Mak

I figured this would happen. I pushed his boundaries, and he tapped out.

"I'm proud of you." Cupping his face, I kiss his forehead.

Carson's on his knees and wraps his arms around me. Anger and panic make him tremble. "Fuck. Fuck, fuck, *fuck!*"

"You did really well," I say, running my fingers through his hair. He's so hot, his skin is clammy. Being touched really is a hard thing for him. Even if he's snuggly and physical every time we're together, I now realize it's because it's been on his terms all along.

He wasn't ready for me to do what I did just now.

He likely thought I was going to spring his dick free and suck him off or something.

But I went for his weak spot, the beast's underbelly, and instead of poking fun at it... I adored it. I cherished it.

Which is what he deserves.

Carson's entire body shakes as he holds me tight. He's not crying, but I think that's only because he's trying his best not to. I would never judge someone for their hangups. We all have them. And in this society, it's almost mandatory that men be strong and not care about their body image.

But it's clear Carson doesn't fit in that mold. He's the most real person I think I've ever met. Hell, even my best friend Leah has struggles that she fakes her way through.

"I'm so sorry," he says once he calms down.

"Don't ever apologize for how you feel, Carson. You did so good with something that's really hard. Be proud of yourself."

He stifles back a groan and tries to stand. I step back to give him space to do so. "Jesus Christ, I can't stop fucking shaking." He runs a trembling hand through his hair, swiping it out of his face. Dropping back on the mattress, he's still struggling to breathe. "I fucking broke." It's like he can't comprehend what just happened. "I can't feel my feet." He snatches me by the waist and holds me again. "I'm so sorry."

"Stop apologizing."

"You deserve better."

Now I'm mad. "You know what I deserve? A man who makes me happy."

"Absolutely."

"*You* make me happy, Carson."

His arms tighten around me. "I'm fucked in the head, Mak. I might make you happy sometimes, but it won't be all the time."

"Well, that's good. I'd hate for life to get boring and predictable."

He chokes out a laugh. "I'm serious."

"So am I." I grip his hair and pull so he has to look up at me. "I deserve someone who will treat me right and loves me for exactly who I am. And so do you." I bend down and kiss him with all my might. It's not sweet and gentle. It's hard and complex and greedy and dominating.

When I break away, he groans and confesses, "I think I'm falling in love with you."

Now it's my turn to freeze on the spot.

"It's too soon for that, I know…" he says. "But I can't get you out of my head, Mak. I tried to back off and give you space, but the two weeks we didn't see each other killed me. I want to spoil you and cherish you and protect you and provide for you. It makes me feel like a fucking caveman."

My heart swoons.

Carson shakes his head. "I've broken every rule I have since the instant I saw your profile on that app. Every. Single. Rule. Mak. It scares me that I've done that."

"Why? Rules should be broken sometimes if the circumstances are right."

He stands and cups my face, holding me even as I step back a little to give him room again. "Rules are there to keep us safe." His brown eyes bore into mine. "To keep *me* safe."

And he broke them all for me.

"I feel like I can be myself with you, Mak, and I can honestly say I've never experienced that in my life. Not even with Lauren."

I don't mind that he's bringing her up again. I suspect she has a lot to do with his past pain. He might not have been enough for her, but he's exactly enough for me.

"It took years of therapy and hard work to get myself to a better headspace. I'm proud of the way I look for the most part, but sometimes I catch myself off guard and the progress I've made vanishes until all I see are the worst pieces of myself. The ones that, no matter how much work I put in, I'll never get rid of."

I'm sure working with models isn't helpful—especially now that I think back to a lot of the covers on his shelf. All those abs. All those "perfect men." I've had some hangups with myself over the years, but for the most part, I accepted my fate and rolled with it. I like myself just as I am.

I want that for Carson too.

Pushing him down on the bed, I crawl on top and straddle him. "Let me love you." I gently kiss his mouth. "Let me show you what your body does to mine." I drag my hands down his chest, feeling his belly quiver when I touch it. "Let me give you everything you've always deserved."

I take off my shirt and bare my heart to him while I wait for his answer.

Chapter 29

Carson

I'm not sure what I did in my life to get the universe to gift me this woman. She once mentioned that her friends called her Mak Truck and I get why. She'll likely plow over your hangups like a semi and drag you along until you either let go or hang on.

I'm hanging on.

With my hands on her hips, I kiss her like my salvation depends on it. I can smell her arousal. Her body doesn't lie. She's been attracted to me from the very beginning—when we stretched together on those stupid yoga mats.

And she's been that way every time we've been together.

She used photos of me to get off with.

She can't keep her hands or gaze off me when we're together.

She uses terms like "Big Boy" as an endearment, and I never once felt like shit hearing it.

I *am* a big boy. I also have a big heart. And Mak's the keeper of it, whether it's against my rules or not.

She slides down my body, peppering it with kisses until she's back to my weak spot. I hold my breath, my gaze locked on hers as my mind scrambles to figure out what she's going to do this time. Relief swarms me when she hooks my waistband with her dainty fingers and tugs my boxers off.

My dick's only a chub because I'm too rattled to think straight.

"Close your eyes," she says, then sucks the head of my cock into her mouth.

I growl. She feels amazing on me. Hot, wet, and hungry—her lips slide up and down my length until I'm fully erect and about to snap. "I love your mouth on me, Mak."

She licks it from base to tip. "I love my mouth on you too." Running her hands across my stomach, I fight the instinct to catch her wrists and stop her. "You have no idea what you do to me, Carson."

My eyes crack open a sliver to look at her again. "Show me."

Mak climbs up my body, leaving another trail of hot kisses in her wake and sits on her throne: My face.

Her panties are soaked. Her scent is mind-bending. Rubbing my nose against the fabric, I love how wet she already is. "This all for me?"

"You better believe it, Big Boy." She straddles my face and pulls her panties to the side. "Feast on it."

I do not have to be told twice.

I lick, suck, and tongue-fuck Mak until she's riding my face. I dig my fingers into her ass cheeks and rock her harder and faster against me. I'm covered in her lust and nearly blow my load with how amazing it is.

"Fuck, don't stop. I'm coming."

I enjoy every second of bringing her closer and closer to a climax. When she bursts, I lick her pussy, groaning as I shove my tongue inside her as deep as I can. I love how her cunt clenches, desperate for my cock to fill her. Rolling her over, my heart's thrashing in my chest, and my dick aches for her hot cunt. She looks at me with a smile that brings my walls crashing down.

That's all the warning I get before she places her feet on my shoulders and shoves back.

"Naughty girl." I growl, my senses all fired up now.

She laughs and tackles me. We wrestle on the bed, rolling all over it until we both fall off. I land on my back and she topples onto me, knocking the air from my lungs.

"Eeek!" She rolls away and crawls on her hands and knees, laughing, toward the bedroom door.

"Where do you think you're going?"

She manages to get to her feet before I have a chance to snag her ankle. Cackle-laughing, she runs out of the room and down my steps, leaving me no choice but to chase after her.

A thrill runs through me.

Clutching the banister, I fly down the steps and into the living room. Mak's on the other side of my couch, panting. Her eyes are wild, smile huge, and pretty body flushed with desire and excitement.

She's so damn beautiful and I'm the reason for the look on her face.

My chest swells with pride. My heart regains its beat.

I stalk towards her, feeling strong and confident.

She flicks her gaze to the sliding glass door then back at me.

"Don't even think about it," I warn her.

Mak bites her bottom lip, and she feints to the left, then right. I rush around to snatch her, but she pivots a third time and leaps over the back of my couch and through the front motherfucking door!

I chase her again and finally manage to tackle Mak on my front lawn.

She squeals and laughs while squirming out of my loose grip. Kicking me in the chest, she dashes out of my hold and runs around the side of my house. I give her a decent head start, marveling at her quickness and long hair flying behind her as she runs away.

Time to catch what's mine.

Shooting off like a rocket, it takes me no time at all to find her in the woods. She's against a tree, out of breath and out of time.

It's freezing out. White clouds puff from her pretty mouth. Steam rises off my body because I'm running hot like usual. I stalk closer, and closer, and closer to her.

Mak gasps when she realizes how close I've just gotten and books it back towards the house.

I catch her just as she's yanking the back sliding glass door open. Spinning her around, I smash my lips to hers and lift her into the air. Aiming my cock to her entrance, I thrust hard and bottom out in one hard thrust. Mak screams into my mouth, and I swallow it. Rocking my hips, I fuck her against the back door, out in the open, with the winter air biting our skin.

Her ass smashes to the glass, and hair falls into my face while I ravage her.

"Don't stop. Please, don't stop." She claws my arms while I hold her up.

"Does my greedy girl want to come around my cock?"

"Yes. Please, yes."

I tug the door open and carry us inside with her still impaled on me. Laying her on the couch, I lift her hips and press my hand to her lower belly. Then I slam into her, feeling my cock slide in and out under my palm.

"Oh my God." Mak tips her head forward

to watch me fuck her like an animal. I'm off my chain and she's the reason.

I take her body like a beast. A ravenous, wild, feral animal whose only reason to be put on this earth is to make this woman come until she can't fucking move.

And that's exactly what I do.

I take her in every position I can possibly think of. She screams my name a dozen times, and I'm so glad I live away from people because the cops would be called on us otherwise. There are red marks on her body where I've grabbed her sweet, perfect skin. There are bite marks on her shoulders and neck.

She's also given me a fair amount of markings herself. I wish each of her bite marks and scratches would last forever.

"That's it. Take my dick like a good girl." I bottom out over and over while she claws at me and arches her back, begging for more.

And more I give her.

I fuck her on the couch, the floor, the steps, my bed, and even the basement. We don't stop until I've chased and fucked her against every surface I own. My thighs are shaking. Sweat drips down my spine. My heart bangs in my throat and still I don't want to stop.

If I stroke out, so be it. This is the only way I want to go.

Once we're in the basement, she rides me on my gaming chair. Mak's hair sticks to her face and back. Her skin's flush and eyes are heavy lidded. Her voice is scratchy each time she says my name. With her feet on my thighs, grip tight on the arms of my chair, she bounces hard and fast on my dick.

"Come for me, Big Boy. Give me everything you fucking have."

Holding her hips, I jackhammer into her pussy, relishing the way my balls tighten while she bounces up and down on my dick. "You want it, come get it." Letting her go, I relinquish all control and tip my head back on the headrest while Mak rides me. "Fuck, I'm close." She feels so goddamn good, I can't hold my release back any longer. At the last second, Mak pops off my dick and I roar. "What are you doing?"

"In my mouth. I want you in my mouth." She drops down to her knees and sucks me off until my fucking eyes cross.

Fisting her hair, I ride a glorious wave of ecstasy that is well-motherfucking-earned. I pump into her mouth while she uses both hands to jerk me until I detonate.

"That's a good boy," she says on her knees after swallowing.

It takes me a moment to catch my breath. I feel dizzy and weak and sleepy and sublime. Gathering her into my arms, I silently get Mak to curl into my lap while we both float down from our highs.

"That was amazing," she whispers. "I've

never been fucked so good in my life."

"Glad I got the honor."

"The honor…" she pants, "was all mine." Mak runs her fingers through my damp hair and kisses me. "I think I wanna keep you."

"I think I wanna keep you, too."

With that, my gaming chair groans, cracks, and collapses with us still in it. We both topple onto the floor, yelling. For a minute, my vision goes white and a sharp pain radiates down my back. "Holy shit, are you okay?"

Mak rolls off me. "I'm good. Are you okay?"

"Yeah. I think so." But the damn chair is in pieces under me. "I almost got pegged again."

Mak laughs so hard she cackles. I've never heard a prettier sound or seen a more beautiful sight in my life.

And that was the moment I knew she'd be mine forever.

Epilogue

Mak

While I'm precariously balanced on the counter, trying to reach the box of dog bones, I hear Carson slam the front door shut.

"What are you doing?" He yells, dropping a box on the kitchen table and rushing over to hold my waist. "Damnit, Mak. I can get you whatever you need. Just ask."

"I'm an independent woman who can reach her own dog bones." That came out weird.

Cooper's tail bangs against the floor while Carson helps me down.

"Who's a good boy?" I toss him a bone.

"Sometimes I can't tell if you're talking to me or the dog."

I scratch Carson's head. "You're a good boy, too."

He growls at me playfully.

I growl right back.

"You got a package."

"Oh yeah?" I grope his dick through his jeans. "Is it the same package you delivered to me this morning, Big Boy?"

"Stop it, you animal." He swats my hand away.

Snatching the box from the table, I have no clue what this could be or how on earth it was delivered here. We've been dating for over a year, and I live a little closer to him now, which is convenient. I spend most nights here with him, and my lease is coming up for renewal soon, so I'm gearing up to have a talk with him about moving in.

"What is this?" I rattle it. "It feels like a book."

"How can that feel like a book? It didn't even jiggle."

"Bookworms know what books feel like. It's instinct." I narrow my gaze suspiciously at him. "I know you know what this is. I can see it on your face."

He continues pretending he has no clue.

Stabbing the box seam with kitchen shears, I tear it open and —

"Oh my God." I carefully pluck out the hardback staring up at me. "Oh my God, oh my God, oh my GOOOODDDDDDD!"

Carson starts laughing. "Pretty good, huh?"

I feel like I'm floating off the floor. The book, with *my face* on the cover, has me utterly speechless. And it takes a lot to make me lose my ability to talk.

It's the cover for that fantasy book Carson

had me take a bath in his studio for. I never asked about it beyond that day, because I didn't want to get my hopes up and then be bummed if the author didn't like the shots Carson took.

"Say something." He stands behind me and wraps his arms around my waist, kissing my neck.

"I... I..." Lifting the book up like it's Simba being presented to the animal kingdom, I can't find the words to express what this does to my little book loving heart. "Am I really this pretty or did Trey have to photoshop the fuck out of it?"

"He didn't touch a damn thing on you. Just tweaked the color of the water to make it more teal and added some weird flowers in the spaces that needed it."

I look like a mystical goddess. "Wow," I whisper. "This is amazing."

He spanks my ass. "You're amazing."

"Trey's amazing, too. This cover is gonna blow up on social media."

"You can tell him so at dinner next week. I made us reservations for next Friday."

"Will Erin be there, too?"

"Of course. And Glitch. And Ara."

Yay! I really like Carson's friends and we don't get to see them very often. It sucks, but that's what video games are for, right? Every week Carson gets on and blasts his conversations so I can join in while curled up on his sofa with a new book and hot tea. And we go out for hot wings with Leah often too. It's the perfect life.

"I have something else for you that just came in," Carson says. Only his voice is a little sharper than it was a moment ago.

He steps away from me, rubbing the back of his neck as he leaves the kitchen without saying another word. I'm not sure if I'm supposed to follow him or not. He returns a minute later with a gift-wrapped box. My brows knit as I stare at it. The dimensions aren't right for another book. And it's too big to be something like a pair of earrings.

"Open it." He steps away and crosses his arms over his chest.

That means he's nervous. What on earth would he be nervous about? Scraping my nails across the paper, I rip off the pretty wrapping and open the lid to a velvet box. There's a silver necklace inside.

"It's a... a collar..." Carson clears his throat. "I had our initials carved into the lock."

My heart thuds hard enough to make me feel dizzy. "What's this mean?"

I think I know, but I want to be sure.

"It means what we both already know, Mak. I'm yours and you're mine. I got a matching one made for me... if you'll have me."

There's no *if* about it. I'll have this man until the day I die. Then I'll crawl into his casket so our bones can turn to dust together. "Can I see yours?"

He pulls a heavier chain out of his front pocket. "I had yours made daintier so it fits your features better."

And Carson's is bigger to fit his.

They're stunning. "Do I get to keep your key?"

"Yes," he says softly.

"Does this mean we're together, for always?"

"The symbolism for something like this ranges in every dynamic, but yeah, Mak." His boots scuff the floor as he draws closer to me. "I want this to be forever."

Tears burn my eyes. Blinking, I set them loose and place the box on the table by the book. "I love it."

"Is that a yes, then?" His tone lifts with what sounds like hope. "Will you wear it for me?"

"Absolutely." I gather my hair up while he takes the necklace with shaky hands and fumbles with the latch twice before he's able to clasp it around my neck and lock it into place. It feels solid against my throat and the tip of my collarbone. "Do people know what this means?"

"If they're familiar with this lifestyle, yes."

"Let me put yours on you." I take it out of his hands and marvel at how heavy it is. Staring at our entwined initials, I honestly can't think of a better way to share a connection with someone. "It's beautiful, Carson."

"I'm glad you like it."

I stand on a chair to put it on his neck. Once it's locked, I run my hands along the backs of his shoulders, loving how firm and big he is. When Carson turns around to face me, I cup his cheeks and kiss him.

This is the best day of my life.

"Better get going." He grips my ass and helps me off the chair. "We have to leave in an hour."

"I have plenty of time to get ready."

"It takes you an hour and a half just to pick out an outfit."

"Because you're constantly taking all my clothes off. I have to make my outfit choices Carson proof."

"Carson proof? Psht. That's not even a thing."

"It should be." I poke his chest. "You tore two of my shirts clean off my body just last weekend."

"I replaced them."

"And my panties?"

"Those were spoils of the hunt." He's not even ashamed.

"And my leggings the week before that?"

"What leggings?"

"The ones you ripped a hole in before fucking me in the ass on the deck."

He holds his chest. "I would never."

Smacking his shoulder, I head out of the kitchen, still laughing.

Carson grabs me before I make it too far and kisses the ever-loving shit out of me. "Move in with me?"

"Okay."

"This weekend?"

"Okay."

"I love you."

"I know." I twist my hips back and forth as I smile up at him. "You were made to love me."

"Fuck right, I am. And you're made to love me."

"You better believe it." Before we fall into each other's arms and miss our reservation, I bristle and flick my hair. "I really must be going now. I'm a very important person. My face is on a book." Waving my hand between us, I tack on, "Call my agent to set up an appointment if you really must speak with me."

Carson roars with laughter as I dash out of the kitchen, and head upstairs to get dressed for tonight. We're going to a sex club. We're fucking in a room full of mirrors. Then we're going camping to hunt, chase, and love each other out in the woods.

I can't believe this is my life.

After I'm dressed, mascara-ed, and have my hair braided, I stare at myself in his mirror to make sure I look okay.

Carson stalks up behind me, shirtless, with his predator gaze locked onto my reflection. "You look beautiful."

"We…" I say, leaning back on him. "*We* look beautiful."

"Yeah," Carson tightens his hold on me. "We definitely do."

I hold my cell phone up and take a selfie of us.

Click.

OTHER BOOKS BY THIS AUTHOR

For information on this book, other books in my
backlist, and future releases,
please visit: **www.BrianaMichaels.com**

If you liked this book, please help spread the
word by leaving a review on the site you
purchased your copy, or on a reader site such as
Goodreads.

I'd love to hear from readers too, so feel free to
send me an email at: sinsofthesidhe@gmail.com
or visit me on Facebook:
www.facebook.com/BrianaMichaelsAuthor

Thank you!

About the Author

Briana Michaels grew up and still lives on the East Coast. When taking a break from the crazy adventures in her head, she enjoys running around with her two children. If there is time to spare, she loves to read, cook, hike in the woods, and sit outside by a roaring fire. She does all of this with the love and support of her amazing husband who always has her back, encouraging her to go for her dreams.